Kaya

Whispers of Love & Scars

HARDIK KEVADIYA

BlueRose ONE
Stories matter
New Delhi • London

BLUEROSE PUBLISHERS
India | U.K.

For permissions requests or inquiries regarding this publication, please contact:

BLUEROSE PUBLISHERS
www.BlueRoseONE.com
info@bluerosepublishers.com
+91 8882 898 898
+4407342408967

ISBN: 978-93-5989-726-4

Cover Design: Sadhna Kumari
Typesetting: Pooja Sharma

First Edition: May 2024

Acknowledgements

Many thanks to people who read the unedited version of the book and provided their points of view and honest feedback about the plots, scenarios and my writing style.

Prologue

Kaya is a breathtaking young woman whose appearance is nothing short of captivating. Her dark, lustrous hair cascades gracefully down her back, a rich contrast to her flawless, porcelain skin. Her eyes, a mesmerizing shade of brown, exude a powerful magnetism, often mirroring the determination within her soul. With an elegance that radiates, she possesses the allure of timeless beauty.

Kaya, a vision of contemporary charm, gracefully weaves tradition into her modern allure through her distinctive attire. Her wardrobe is proof of a perfect fusion of cultural richness and a chic, contemporary vibe. One cannot help but be captivated by the subtle elegance she exudes.

A dark black bindi adorns her forehead, reminiscent of a precious gem. It serves as an accessory and a nod to tradition, bestowing her an enchanting aura. This small yet significant detail becomes a defining feature of her distinctive style.

The traditional earrings she wears, known as "Jhumkas," dangle gracefully from her ears. Each piece tells a story of timeless grace, with their gentle sway mirroring the rhythmic cadence of her every step. These jhumkas are more than mere adornments, become carriers of heritage and echoes of a rich cultural legacy.

Her personality is a brilliant blend of charisma, compassion and strength. She is a young girl in her early twenties who has been shaped by her upbringing, embodying kindness, empathy and a soft-spoken demeanor that sets her apart. Her maturity is well beyond her years, she showcases captivating wisdom.

Kaya embodies the virtues of diligence and determination, serving as a commendable example of self-reliance. Her commitment to achieving her aspirations is evident in her strong work ethic, making her a role model for those who value hard work over dependency. Instead of relying on others, Kaya actively invests effort, reflecting her inclination towards self-sufficiency.

Demonstrating a grounded and responsible nature, she consistently showcases her compassion and exhibits authenticity in her actions. Her unique blend of internal and external beauty beautifully reflects her Gujarati heritage, portraying her as a graceful and sensual individual.

Her transformation from a reserved personality to a confident, self-assured woman is a journey that, while not uncommon, remains extraordinary. Noteworthy is her boldness in taking initiative, such as orchestrating a meeting with me, underscoring her evolving character that continues to captivate those acquainted with her.

She has always been more mature than any other girl of her age. Her upbringing molded her into a kind, sympathetic and soft-spoken girl. She was flawless. She was the middle of three daughters living with her parents in Ahmedabad city. Her younger sister was still in high school and her elder sister married last year. Her father was working in one of the biggest textile factories in Ahmedabad.

Her father had done his best to provide the best possible education to all three sisters. She loved her sisters, mother and father more than anyone else. Her family was her strength and weakness both at the same time. She was allowed to work, but convincing her father took almost one and a half years. She wanted a scooter, but rather than demanding a scooter from her father, she chose to work and earn money. I wasn't lying when I said that she was self-reliant.

She took the bus from near the office along with some colleagues and girlfriends from the office. She always worked in the first shift 6:00 a.m. to 3:00 p.m., which was common for girls working in a call center.

It doesn't matter what time you look at her; you will always find her fresh, like she just came out after taking a shower, with a gentle smile on her soft pink lips and shiny, long black hair. Her slim yet curvy figure was captivating, driving boys around her crazy. I was no different; I was and am crazy for her.

Kaya's smile was like a moonbeam on a night, illuminating everything around her. Her passion for life is like a whirlwind of emotions that envelops you in a warm and passionate embrace. Her intelligence is like an ancient book filled with knowledge, with every page revealing a new mystery, yet a lighthouse in the storm, guiding everyone safely through life's turbulent waters.

Contents

A Kiss

I was exhausted after the day's labor at 4:00 a.m., but I still had one more chore to complete. I was drafting my last report summary email to my manager when my phone began to buzz. Her message was a good morning greeting. Every day, she sent good morning and good night texts like clockwork. Many of my teammates did the same; it was usual for people to send messages to colleagues and family members. This tendency has resulted from the cheap cost of text message charges. Many people sent out messages to their full contact list before their daily allotment expired at midnight. Most morning greetings get ignored, but her message unexpectedly drew a response from me. Futility blurred my usual protocols, or I needed a distraction. I'd been buried in work since 12:15 a.m., a smoking break after my last update to the manager serving as the only break in four hours. It was usual for me to work late hours, but the month ends were grueling.

I worked in a call center as a team leader; preparing monthly reports for my team and sending them to my manager was one of my daily responsibilities, but month ends were a completely different story. The team leaders in the evening shift always compiled and sent the department's attendance report to the human resource team.

I had already compiled the report and was writing the summary in an email to my manager when her message distracted me.

"good morning!" I replied, kept my mobile phone aside and started writing the email. I had just written a few words and my phone vibrated again.

It was a message from her. "Why are you still up?" she had asked.

"I am finishing my monthly reporting and will be done in the next few minutes," my message to her response read. I wasn't expecting any message from her after my good morning message, but she continued and so did I, for the first time. Before I could put my mobile aside, my mobile vibrated once more.

"Are you still in the office?" she asked.

"Yeah," my simple message to her read. I plugged a charging cable into my mobile and started writing the email to my manager. I was reading the email one last time before hitting send and my phone vibrated again.

"I will be in the office by 5:00; please wait for me," her message read.

It was the first of the month, so I checked the new roster of her work times. She usually worked the early morning shift from 6:00 a.m. to 3:00 p.m. and she worked the first shift from 7:00 a.m. to 4:00 p.m. For a few months, the team member who worked the early morning shift wished to transfer to the mid-shift.

I had accomplished a lot at the age of twenty-two. Before graduating from college, I worked as a team leader at a prominent contact center in the city, managing a team of twenty-five people. When I started my first year of college, I began working. Working in a contact center gave me easy access to money; I didn't have to beg to my parents for money. I was attending a government institution therefore, my two-month pay from the job paid my complete year's tuition. "Why?" I sent her a message, kept my mobile aside and returned to writing the email. In the next few minutes, I finished my work and sent the report to my manager; after checking my inbox before shutting down my computer, I headed to the office cafeteria for a smoke.

I bought a cup of tea and had my cigarette and tea, thinking why she wanted me to wait for her. It was the first time in months that we exchanged messages. I couldn't come up with an explanation for her request. If I were to describe it to someone else, we were not buddies - she was someone I knew from my office. We both worked in the same office and department. Our department has more than 1,200 employees, making it impossible to know everyone at a personal level.

Whenever the opportunity presented itself, I put myself within a ten-meter radius of her. I liked her but never dared to approach her for two reasons: firstly, she was amongst the most beautiful girls in the office and secondly, team leader dating an employee in the same department was considered a red flag for promotions. Her presence in the office naturally gravitated me towards her. It would be wild to imagine her as my girlfriend, though. I was just another average boy in the office. After finishing my tea and cigarette, I returned to the office floor. The office had four floors with a closed cafeteria and an open smoking area on a terrace.

Reaching my desk, I started packing my bag with a plan to head home. The floor's main door beeped; someone swiped their access card to get the entry. I took a side step, trying to see who it was. It was her, Kaya.

"Wait for 10 minutes, please," she said while rushing to the floor pantry area, "I want to talk to you." Before I could ask her anything, she ran towards the back of the office.

My shift started at 3:00 p.m., but I used to reach the office a little early so that I could catch up with my friends and colleagues from the morning shifts and when possible, just look at her before she left for home. Usually, I only had a few minutes before I could catch up with my friends and colleagues and I could find her in the crowd of five hundred people working on the floor and stalk her from afar. She logged out at 4:00 p.m.

A few months back, I worked the morning shift for a week. I was forced to take the morning shift to help my friend and colleague Payal. She was not only a friend and a colleague, but also used to be my team leader during my calling days and my mentor when I was learning the responsibilities of a team leader. I had spent hundreds of hours shadowing her work and she had taught me every nook and cranny of being a high-performing team leader. Payal was also a firecracker; not even senior managers dared to cross her and other team leaders never messed with her or her team members. She was like a teacher and a big sister at the same time, we shared the last name "Patel," which helped us create a stronger bond. So, when she asked for a favor, I couldn't say no. Even if I wanted to say no, I never dared.

That week, at 5:45 in the morning, I was standing outside our office gate smoking a cigarette. A bus passed and I heard a crowd talking and rushing from behind me to the office gate. I stepped aside, giving them easy access to the entrance. I finished and headed inside the office.

The first thing in a call center you do is to take updates before you can start your day. It was mandatory and important. A briefing to keep ourselves updated with the new promotion launched by the corporate marketing team, learning about any changes to the existing products or any new products launched in the region. If a customer calls and inquires about any of them, call center executives should be able to answer them swiftly and accurately.

I summoned everyone at my desk for a briefing and within a minute I had more than twenty team members gathered around me. After about fifteen minutes, everyone returned to their workstations. I began promoting attendance, reviewed the roster for that day and began following up with team members who had yet to report to the office. We kept a file containing contact information for everyone in our department in case we wanted to reach them. I phoned a team member who had been scheduled to be at the office at 6:00 a.m. but was late. After numerous failed tries, I moved on to the next. I spoke with several boys and girls who had arrived late that morning. A girl walked in the gate and stood near my desk. I was on the phone following up with the rest of the team members from the roster.

"Sir, briefing," she said timidly.

I don't know if she was tired after running or scared of me, but she was timid. Her voice was low, making it difficult to hear her. Thanks to the early morning silence, I could understand what she said. I asked for her name to mark her attendance on the roster.

"Kaya," she replied.

It was then I learned about a girl named "Kaya." I had heard that name several times in the evening shifts, a beautiful girl who had rejected many boys from our and other departments. She was the one who was denying boys left, right and center. She was more beautiful than people described her, not doing justice to her beauty.

A week passed quickly and I returned to my normal shift hours. I liked working in the evening shifts and had worked in the evenings for the entirety of my two-and-a-half years of tenure working there. I enjoyed my time with my colleagues and friends from the evening shifts.

Working the evening shift meant no fear of the managers and clients walking on the floor after 07:00 p.m., Making us team leaders the second highest in command for over five hundred boys. Working without the supervision of a manager meant power to us. We could dictate what we do and when we do it. The same office had another atmosphere in the evening hours. The most experienced yet disobedient and troublesome delinquent worked in the evening hours. You could learn everything that happened that morning on any other floor in the office from those bunch. They had maintained their communication channel under the nose of the IT department without even realizing it.

"Wait for just ten minutes, please. I want to talk to you," Kaya said before rushing to the floor pantry.

"Okay, okay!" I agreed. I was tired and wanted to go home.

After packing my bag, I sat there for almost ten minutes, waiting for her to return to the floor. Instead of her coming to the floor, she texted on my phone.

"Come to the pantry, please."

Thinking why she was asking me to come to the pantry, I walked to the back of the office, where the pantry area was located. I walked into the office pantry and saw Kaya standing there.

She wore a white sleeveless dress that hugged her curves perfectly. Her long black hair moved to her back as she walked towards me. She had a red *bindi* on her forehead, which added a touch of sensuality to her look.

I couldn't tear my gaze away; she stood before me, the embodiment of beauty. Her physique boasted perfection, adorned with curves that gracefully accentuated her silhouette. Smooth, flawless skin adorned her frame, her eyes sparkled with an inexplicable allure and her lips, now adorned with a creamy red lipstick, were irresistibly inviting. A deep breath was necessary to calm my racing heart as I realized the importance of making a lasting impression.

A subtle change had occurred and after careful observation, I identified the difference – her lips, usually adorned in a natural light pink hue, were now enhanced with the elegance of creamy red lipstick.

Unable to contain my admiration, I complimented her, "You look stunning, Kaya. What's the special occasion?" The early morning found us alone in the office, Kaya having arrived well before the commencement of the first shift.

Closing the physical and metaphorical distance between us, Kaya leaned in. Her brown, soulful eyes sought mine for any indication of consent. Before my mind could comprehend the significance of the moment, her lips akin to a whisper of temptation, delicately brushed against mine.

Initially taken aback, my heart raced and my thoughts momentarily froze. Caught in a powerful vortex of confusion and desire, I struggled to process the reality that the woman I had admired from a distance was sharing this intimate moment with me. A momentary hesitation lingered, the world seemingly halting around us. Kaya's kiss: sweet and tantalizing, became a spark that ignited my senses and awakened dormant desires.

In that instant, my initial shock morphed into an overwhelming rush of emotion. Closing my eyes, I let go of lingering reservations, allowing my lips to respond to the allure of Kaya's kiss. It was a kiss characterized by vulnerability and surrender, a moment where the barriers encasing our hearts crumbled away.

It felt like our lips met with an electric intensity, a firework display of emotions that left both of us breathless. As we deepened the kiss, I realized I had water in my eyes I did not know what it was then; I had found love, passion, intimacy and the courage to embrace it.

It was a kiss that changed our lives, sealing our connection and igniting a love that would burn brighter with every passing day.

It was just over a minute, but it felt like time had stopped running and we had lived many hours in those few minutes.

"Are you crying?" she asked. "No," I replied, wiping my tears and cleaning my watery eyes.

I don't know what it was, but I could hear my heartbeat; my chest was heavy, but surprisingly, it felt amazing. I was overwhelmingly excited and happy. It was my first kiss with a girl I secretly liked I still don't know why I had tears in my eyes.

"On your next week off, can we go on a movie date?" She suddenly asked.

"What was that just now?" I replied to her question with my own, ignoring her question.

"A kiss. I kissed you because I wanted to. For a while now, actually." She answered without any hesitation and with confidence. The timid Kaya I knew from a few months back had been long gone. I was surprised by her confidence and directness. Deep down in my heart, I liked what she had just said.

I had never kissed or dated before, nor had a girl asked me for a movie. It was all new for me, but I was excited and happy; I nodded, "Yes."

She kissed me on my cheeks before she went out on the floor. I followed her to the floor, promised to text her and said goodbye.

I drove my motorcycle toward my home, thinking of what had happened, smiling, imagining our next meeting; I was parking at my house before I knew it. My ride home felt shorter that day.

"Good night." I sent her a message before going to bed.

"Good night ♥" My mobile rang; I tried to content myself and keep my emotions in check. What happened in the last few hours was all surreal.

From that day, messaging Kaya and replying to her messages was second nature to me. A few days passed by texting, flirting with secrets and exchanging innocent smiles in the office that only we could understand. I was confident that we were careful in the office so nothing was out of place and we could carry on like colleagues.

Vijay, my colleague and a good friend, like a dog he was, had sniffed the roses in the air. That evening, on a smoking break, he asked, "When did you both start dating?"

My heart skipped a heartbeat and I flustered; the puff I just had left a sensation in my throat. "How did you know?" I stopped coughing, cleared my throat and asked Vijay.

"Jerk, you think you can keep it a secret from me," he replied.

I shared with him the essence of what had unfolded between Kaya and me in recent days, assuring him that I would divulge all the details when we had more time. Despite his agreement, he couldn't resist venting his frustration, subjecting me to a barrage of curses and abuse throughout the day. It was evident that this onslaught would persist until I laid bare all the facts.

However, there was one aspect of our story that I held back — the morning of our first kiss. That moment held a special place in my heart and I intended to keep it shielded from prying eyes. With the weight of confessions off our shoulders, Kaya and I stood on the brink of a new beginning. The days that followed felt like an exciting adventure waiting to unfold.

As Kaya and I delved into texting each other, each message became a small revelation, offering a glimpse into the other's world. My phone would illuminate with a message and my heart would involuntarily skip a beat at the sight of Kaya's name. Our conversations flowed effortlessly, resembling a gentle river meandering through topics ranging from our school and college experiences to discussions about friends and family members.

Every interaction with Kaya felt like unwrapping a new layer of intimacy and the anticipation of what the next message might reveal became a delightful part of my routine. Our connection deepened as we explored various facets of our lives, fostering a bond built on curiosity, genuine interest and the shared joy of discovering one another.

I learned that Kaya was an avid reader, just like me. But our interests were completely different; I liked comics and stories and she liked books based on real stories. Our shared passion for reading created a special bond between us. Sometimes, we'd stay up late, texting about the characters we loved and the plots that had touched our hearts. We often imagine ourselves as a character from books, especially superheroes and characters from love stories.

Our conversations soon turned playful. We teased each other, exchanged jokes and even exchanged fantasies about what we read or sometimes watched; often, it felt like we were trading smiles and laughter in the same room. Kaya had a knack for making me smile and I had a way of bringing out her more relaxed, humorous side.

Before we knew it, Saturday was here and it was my week off. The day I was about to go on my first movie date with Kaya. I had butterflies in my stomach the whole afternoon. I stopped by the saloon, got a haircut and had my beard trimmed. I cleaned my white shoes while thinking of the unfathomable moments I planned to create and experience. I played out scenarios of walking by her side, holding her hands, talking to her, watching a movie and having dinner. I tried to imagine what she would be thinking and planning. We never discussed what she wanted to do after the film and dinner.

I had assumed she would have some restrictions from her family that she had to follow, so I wasn't expecting anything other than a movie.

My phone rang and I thought it was her. I was wrong; Vijay advised me to buy the protection, just in case.

"Buzz off," I replied.

The very next minute, my phone rang once more. I thought it was Vijay with something crazy to add. Once more, I needed to be corrected. It was Kaya.

"Meet me at the movie theater near our office at 5:00 p.m.," her message stated.

After we started secretly dating, Kaya changed her shift timings from 6:00 a.m. to 10:00 a.m. to spend more time in the office together. Even though we kept it professional, Vijay sometimes caught me exchanging smiles and blinking eyes at Kaya.

I was surprised when she asked me to meet her at 5:00 p.m. instead of 8:00 p.m. The movie tickets I bought were for eight o'clock. I wasn't aware that she took a half-day from work; it was nearly impossible to get unplanned half-days on weekdays. Half-day on weekdays required prior approval from our manager.

I was busy thinking why she had asked me to meet her earlier than planned and my mobile rang, “Your girlfriend just left.” Vijay texted.

I smiled for two reasons: she left the office and I would meet her sooner than planned and even though Vijay was the biggest pain in the butt, he cared for me as a brother.

"I'm on my way," I messaged Kaya. I rode my motorcycle to the planned location, but driving just twelve kilometers felt like a thousand. After 25 minutes of navigating the heavy traffic in Ahmedabad city, I finally arrived at the location near the construction site of the riverfront project in the city's center. I began searching for her and eventually spotted her waiting beneath a tree on the side of the road. I called out her name, "Kaya," and she turned towards my voice. I quickly parked my motorcycle and rushed to her.

It was our first date and we were meeting outside the office for the first time. Kaya looked at me with a smile and I smiled back. There was a brief moment of silence between us, which felt awkward. We had been messaging a lot but had never talked on the phone and just now met outside the office for the first time.

“Why did you take a half-day and how did you get the approval from the office?” I gathered the strength, cleared my voice and asked her.

She smiled and replied, “It was easy; I told Payal I had my period and she approved my half-day.”

“Is it?” I asked and she said “No” before I could finish my two-part question.

We laughed and the rest of the evening was filled with effortless conversation. That laugh was the perfect icebreaker. That day, I discovered a completely new characteristic of Kaya's personality. She was mature, kind-hearted, soft spoken but also witty, bubbly and willful.

"Let's take a walk," she said.

We had almost two and a half hours before our movie, so we walked. As we walked, we talked and got to know each other better. It was refreshing to hear her voice instead of imagining it through messages. After walking, I suggested we find a place to sit and chat. I wanted to take in every detail of her appearance without distractions from the busy road we were walking through.

She looked most beautiful in my eyes when she wore a white dress and on our first date, she was in white. She looked more radiant and self-assured than before.

With every joyous laugh, our conversations drew us closer as if a magnetic force was pulling us together. The phrase "I like" became a recurring melody in our discussions, carrying an undeniable electricity that fueled our growing fondness. Kaya had a broader range of topics to discuss than I did and her conversation was more playful and flirtatious. It was as if she was sharing all the fascinating stories she had read and every topic she talked about brought us one step closer.

My heart skipped a beat as she touched and clapped my hands. "Am I boring you?" Kaya asked.

"Never," I replied immediately with a smile.

"Why don't you talk? I will listen and keep looking at you," she suggested, looking into my eyes.

Perched on a bench, a palpable sense of anticipation enveloped us. Her brown eyes, locked onto mine, conveyed a myriad of emotions, creating an unspoken dialogue between us. The exchange of glances towards each other's lips hung in the air, an implicit question lingering, felt with profound intensity. Amidst the bustling riverfront and crowded sidewalk, we existed in our cocoon, as if the universe had conspired to grant us this intimate moment.

Her eyes, a deep brown, held an inexplicable allure, drawing me in with a magnetic force. Engulfed in the depth of her gaze,

I ventured to steal glances at her lips, recognizing the unspoken agreement for a kiss that lingered tantalizingly between us.

As I inched closer, so did she, our proximity allowing me to absorb the warmth of her breath. Although our lips nearly touched, the prospect of a public kiss on the bustling sidewalk restrained our actions. We were acutely aware that such displays of affection in public could pose challenges for us, a topic we had dissected during our midnight conversations.

Resisting the magnetic pull required more effort and self-discipline than initially envisioned. Despite the tantalizing temptation, we both understood the potential risks. In those times, it had become commonplace for foreigners to face fines for public displays of affection and the looming threat of a complaint for engaging in an "obscene act" kept us grounded. The unspoken promise of a kiss remained suspended in the air, a testament to our shared understanding of the need for discretion in the face of societal norms.

“Let’s head back; it is almost time for a movie,” I said.

"Yes," Kaya nodded her head. I held her hand and we both headed towards my motorcycle. As we embarked on our motorcycle ride toward the theater, the thrill of the open road blended with our palpable excitement for the date. Kaya sat gracefully behind me, her knees gently grazing my legs with no space for air to pass between us. The warmth of her presence and proximity sent shivers down my spine. Every turn of the road seemed to resonate with our shared adventure and the wind promised an unforgettable evening. The engine's sound harmonized with the rhythmic beating of our hearts as we navigated the path ahead, setting the stage for a movie night that would be etched in our memories forever.

We arrived at the theater in just a few minutes. I parked my motorcycle and we made our way towards the lift. After a little while, we reached the theater hall and started climbing towards our seats. Kaya had chosen the movie and asked for specific seats in a certain row. The evening we had been looking forward to was finally here, our long-anticipated movie date.

As we approached our seats, my heart raced with expectation. I couldn't help but steal glances at her in the theater while passing her to get to my seat, a flutter of nerves mixing with eagerness.

As we settled down, a soft hum of anticipation filled the air. The classic movie echoed our journey, paying tribute to the timeless love stories that had come before. She had chosen a seat in the middle of the top row, providing us with an uninterrupted view of the screen.

The movie began, but the real magic happened in the gaps between the scenes. Our hands brushed each other, exchanging knowing glances in the dim light. The screen seemed like a backdrop to the story unfolding between us.

Amid a suspenseful movie scene, our fingers naturally intertwined, sparking a surge of electricity that coursed through both of us. On the back of Kaya's hand, I traced gentle circles, a subtle yet meaningful expression of my affection for her. In response, Kaya leaned in, finding a comfortable spot to rest her head on my shoulder. The warmth emanating from her and the rhythmic beat of her heartbeat formed an ethereal connection that seemed to transcend the constraints of time and space. At that moment, the world outside ceased to exist.

Our eyes met in a shared understanding, exchanging a gaze that conveyed the emotions that had been building up over the past week. It was as if the universe had momentarily paused, allowing this profound connection to flourish. While other couples in the theater were lost in passionate kisses, we remained in our bubble, enveloped in an unspoken agreement.

The desire to kiss Kaya surged within me, but a lingering concern about appearing overly eager held me back. I grappled with the internal debate, recognizing the thin line between expressing affection and avoiding the label of a desperate boyfriend. In that suspended moment, I chose to hold back, savoring the closeness we shared without rushing into a gesture that might overshadow the genuine connection we were cultivating.

The climax of the movie was a perfect reflection of what was happening between Kaya and me. As the tension peaked on the screen, I slowly raised Kaya's chin and kissed her. It took me a lot of courage to make the first move, but I was glad I made it. Kaya responded with an emotional heart, her lips meeting mine in a passionate, soul-stirring kiss. Our hearts were beating together, a symphony of emotions, a crescendo of love and desire that erupted in that moment. We lost ourselves in each other and the people around us seemed to disappear. We knew that others sitting next to us could see and were staring at us; we acted as if we didn't care. Our kiss was filled with yearning built up between us. It was a daring move I wouldn't have done in a public place like a road, but a closed movie theater was another story. The more experienced couples kissing in the theater encouraged me to do so.

As the credits rolled and we left the movie theater, holding hands, the excitement of our first date remained. Our connection had deepened more than ever and we couldn't keep our hands off each other. We stopped at a quiet bench in the moonlit parking lot and our lips met again in a series of tender kisses. Our love was like a melody, with each kiss blending into the next, forming a passionate and timeless symphony. We paused occasionally, our eyes locked, our breaths mingling, silently affirming the love we shared. Our kisses were an unspoken promise, a vow to explore the beautiful chapters of our love story together, one tender, breathless kiss at a time.

She expressed her affections once again, her words filled with tenderness. It promised more beautiful moments, a bond that had grown more profound throughout our movie date.

"I like you," she whispered with a pure smile.

Whenever she smiled, my heart skipped a beat. How could she be so innocent and yet cunning at the same time? Kaya had a mischievous side; her sudden kiss in the office pantry was one of those deviant acts. Many boys from our office approached her, but she had turned down every one of them.

"I love you," I responded to her right ear.

"I know," she said.

As I drove from the parking lot to the main street, she bit me twice on my back.

Her place added just a few kilometers of diversion to my ride home. "Let me drop you off and then I'll go home," I asked.

"Why? Can't we go somewhere else?" She replied.

I would be lying if I said I had not considered spending a night with her. In my head, I had played hundreds of scenarios of us being intimate that night. I had the whole morning and afternoon to think about it. On top of that, what had transpired that evening and her biting my back had given me the cues that she wanted more than just kisses.

"Where do you want to go? A hotel or my friend's place." I rushed without thinking about anything else at that moment.

"Over there!" She grabbed my jaw and pointed in the direction.

How I could not know there was a hotel nearby, I thought while my eyes looked for any boards or signs of the hotel. Vijay had already overloaded me with the names of all the safe hotels I should use.

"Ice cream parlor, you idiot." She shouted while stomping my feet.

With her sudden outburst, I couldn't help but chuckle and after feeling a bit embarrassed, I chose to act as a saint.

"Oh, an ice cream parlor! Of course, how could I not know that?" I said with a faux expression of surprise.

As I drove in the direction she had pointed, we began a playful banter about my supposed inability to think of an ice cream parlor. The laughter was contagious when we finally arrived at the ice cream parlor. We both walked in, still smiling and examined the myriad flavors on display. As I took my time selecting the perfect scoop, she continued to make light-hearted remarks about me thinking of a hotel instead of an ice cream parlor.

Once I had my ice cream, I found a cozy corner in the parlor and as we both enjoyed our treats, our playful exchange continued. The ice cream quickly became a symbol of our shared amusement, turning what could have been an awkward situation into a delightful, memory-making moment.

I dropped her off at her place. Before she could get away from my reach for the night, I stopped her and we exchanged a small but much-needed kiss. I didn't have to ask for it like she had read my mind.

"I love you," she said and rushed towards her gate without allowing me to say it back.

I started driving to my place, smiling and thinking about my evening with Kaya.

"Fish!" I shouted while driving. I realized that Kaya had said that she loved me and not that she liked me. This was the first time she had said that she loved me. Some will argue that there is not much difference, but for me, it was a difference as vast as day and night.

Nowhere to be Found

It's been over two years since I last talked with Kaya; she had broken the promises we made. What I assumed was the beginning of lifelong happiness had turned into a lifelong emptiness. My heart was full of anger, confusion, frustration and pain. I started losing focus on my work and lost touch with my colleagues in the morning shift. Only a handful of friends and colleagues knew the whole situation. Vijay, Anjali and Payal were among them.

Vijay tried to cheer me up whenever he could, but it wasn't easy. Later, I learned that Vijay had asked our manager to move his shift similar to mine so he could spend more time with me in the office. One late evening, during a cigarette break in the office terrace, I sat across from Vijay. I have been telling him about Kaya and how much I missed her. As I started speaking, my voice began to tremble and my eyes went up with tears.

Vijay reached across the table and took my hand. "It's okay, brother," he said. "You can cry."

I nodded and the tears started to fall. I cried softly at first, but then my sobs became more uncontrollable. Vijay sat there quietly, listening to me cry and offering comfort in his silence. I cried for Kaya and for the love that I had lost. I cried because of the pain and the loneliness that I was feeling. As I cried sitting there, Vijay squeezed my shoulder. He didn't speak a word, but his silence was more comforting than any words could be. When I stopped crying, I wiped my eyes and looked at Vijay.

"I'm so sorry; I didn't mean to break down like that," I said.

"It's okay," Vijay replied. "You needed to cry. It's good to let it out."

Vijay and I sat silently for a moment, both lost in thought. Then, Vijay stood up.

"I'm going to get us some more tea," he said. "Do you want anything else?"

I shook my head. "No, I'm fine."

Vijay nodded and walked away. I sat there and watched him go, grateful for his understanding and friendship. After he returned, we continued with our work for the day and went home.

Messaging Kaya has become my daily ritual. I only had one photo of her, which I had found in our office records; the rest I had were her memories. I messaged Anjali, a colleague at our office, who knew about our relationship and held a deep trust within Kaya's family. She had connections to them and had often spent time at Kaya's home, her friendship extending beyond the boundaries of the workplace. With a heavy heart, I approached Anjali, explaining the circumstances that had left me in emotional turmoil. Anjali, too, had been concerned about Kaya's abrupt departure. Still, her attempts to reach out had met with the same impenetrable silence. She, like me, felt helpless and anxious about Kaya's well-being.

She agreed to visit Kaya's home. She knocked on the door, hoping to see Kaya or her family, but each attempt ended in frustration as the house remained unresponsive. The situation was deeply disconcerting and our shared concern grew with each unsuccessful visit

During one of Anjali's visits, a compassionate neighbor in Kaya's building unraveled the mystery that had perplexed us for so long. With a heavy heart, the neighbor revealed the heartbreaking truth – Kaya's younger sister had tragically passed away. The news was a seismic blow, not only to me but also to Anjali. The profound loss had upheaved the foundations of Kaya's family, prompting them to make a poignant decision. They withdrew from the city, seeking solace in their village, where they cocooned themselves in grief for their departed daughter and sister. Even Kaya's elder sister, who was married, had temporarily joined them in their ancestral home for a few months.

The revelation left me grappling with a surge of emotions. I couldn't fathom the depth of pain Kaya must have endured, mourning the loss of her sister. Regret gnawed at me as I realized I had been ignorant of her silent struggles, harboring unnecessary anger instead of providing the support she desperately needed.

The desire to reach out to Kaya surged within me, but the fear of rejection and exacerbating her pain held me back. I opted to respect her need for time and space, hoping she would initiate contact when she felt ready.

In the following months, my determination to reconnect with Kaya persisted. Frustration mounted as my calls and messages went unanswered, leaving me with an overwhelming sense of isolation and rejection. Determined to bridge the growing chasm, I resorted to waiting outside Kaya's residence, a desperate attempt to catch a glimpse of her and understand the turmoil she was grappling with.

Despite my relentless efforts, Kaya remained elusive, secluded within the walls of her silent world. The ache of isolation became unbearable and my yearning to see her and offer support intensified. It was during this challenging period that Anjali called, summoning me to the bus stop near the office. Hope and anticipation welled up within me, eager to hear news about Kaya's well-being.

I rushed to the bus stop. "So, what's the news?" I asked her while sitting beside her.

"I'm so sorry," she replied.

"What is it?" I asked with hesitation and fear.

"Kaya doesn't want you to contact her anymore." She mentioned with her head down.

"But...why?" I asked.

"I don't know." She didn't say anything. Anjali replied. "I don't understand either and I know It's unfair to you."

I felt so lost and could not speak anything else. Anjali's words hit me like a heavy blow and the lack of explanation or clarity only deepened the mystery surrounding Kaya's disappearance.

I was torn between my desire to respect Kaya's wishes and my need to understand her situation and be there for her during her darkest times. It was a torment I couldn't escape, a battle between my desires and fear of causing her more pain. My heart ached with the struggle, but I could do nothing for her. I felt completely useless and lost.

The next day, in the office, Anjali came to my desk and asked if we could talk for a few minutes. She said she could not tell the entire thing yesterday and wanted me to listen to her.

Anjali's news about Kaya's father was truly heart-wrenching. It added to the already-existing mystery and silence between Kaya and me. Kaya's father had taken an unprecedented step, severely impacting their family's communication ability.

Kaya's father, who had always been a pillar of strength for their family, decided to remove her mobile phone and cut off her connection with the outside world. This decision was motivated by the deep grief that had consumed their family and his unwavering love for his daughters. It was a drastic step to protect their family from the pain that seemed to be coming at them from all directions.

As I listened to Anjali's story, I could hear the trembling in her voice as she recounted the weighty revelation. The thought of Kaya's father, once a pillar of strength, now consumed by grief, weighed heavily on my heart. The gravity of his sorrow was impossible to ignore and the weight of his silence was profound.

The neighbors had seen how Kaya's father, who was once full of life, became a mere shadow of his former self. He had retreated from everything and everyone and his voice was silent because of his overwhelming grief. It had been several months since anyone had heard him speak and his silence was a testament to the agony that had taken hold of his soul.

It was evident that Kaya's father had a deep affection for his youngest daughter. Her loss devastated their family and left an enduring impact on the man who had raised her. The weight of his sorrow was beyond words and his pain left an indelible mark on all acquainted with him.

The revelation complicated Kaya's disappearance, deepening the mystery and evoking mixed emotions: sadness, compassion and a desire for support.

As I reflected on the profound sorrow felt by the family, my thoughts turned to the father. This man had once adored his youngest daughter, whose laughter had once filled their home. Now, he was a captive of his agony. His silence spoke volumes, amplifying the torment that had befallen their family.

As the months passed, it became increasingly clear that Kaya's silence was not just a passing phase. It had become a part of her new reality and I needed to respect her need for space, even if it meant letting go of the person I had cared for deeply. But amid the heartache and uncertainty, one memory remained etched in my mind. It was a memory that reminded me of the joyous night we had shared.

One night, while we were messaging, I remembered she had thrown me a playful dare. She dared me to meet her at her apartment, promising a kiss and anything else I desired. She had questioned if I could reach her home within 15 minutes from when she sent me the message.

"I won't let you change your mind," I messaged determinedly, setting off on my impromptu adventure.

I was already near her gate before time ran out. I quickly messaged her and asked her to meet me in her apartment parking. The excitement was building and the prospect of the challenge had made me smile.

As I stood by the elevator, the air buzzed with anticipation. When Kaya emerged, her attire radiated a simple yet captivating elegance – a light pink T-shirt paired with white shorts. Her hair, usually cascading freely, was neatly tied in a bun, showcasing a different side of her beauty. That evening marked the first time I saw her without the customary *bindi*, an omission that only enhanced her allure.

Unable to resist, I drew her close, planting a gentle kiss on her forehead as she approached. It was a subtle reminder that I had met her challenge, arriving within the 15-minute window she had dared me to achieve.

"Why the forehead?" she teased. "I said I'd let you kiss me if you made it in 15 minutes."

I smiled, responding, "You promised me a kiss and I just claimed that one."

In a playful response, she clung to my neck and, with a smile, planted a sweet kiss on my left cheek. Laughter and happiness filled the moment, a testament to the chemistry we shared.

Six months of relentless pursuit had taken a toll, prompting a realization that Kaya needed her space and her unique way of navigating the challenges life had thrown at her. The constant uncertainty and repeated rejections had led me to a point of surrender.

My friends and colleagues, witnesses to my struggle – individuals like Payal, Vijay and Anjali – had implored me to consider moving forward. To relinquish the incessant yearning and the unanswered questions.

Ultimately, I made the arduous decision to cease reaching out, releasing the threads that bound us to the past. I chose to no longer utter her name in my conversations as if deciding to erase a chapter of my life and act as if I had never known a girl named Kaya. It was a painful yet necessary choice, one that underscored my respect for her autonomy and the path she had chosen.

It was a painful process, a decision made not out of indifference but out of love and respect. It was a recognition that sometimes, to care for someone truly, you must let them find their way, even if it means leaving a part of your heart behind. I moved on, not because I had stopped loving her, but because I loved her enough to respect her need for space and silence.

The pain didn't disappear and the questions remained unanswered. But I had taken the first step toward healing, allowing Kaya to find her path and accepting that sometimes, love means letting go. I decided to cherish the moments we had created and spend the rest of my life hoping our paths would eventually intervene, making me feel alive again.

As the days turned into weeks, my resolve to move on from Kaya remained steadfast. I had stopped talking about her, following the advice of friends and colleagues who had encouraged me to take that necessary step. The decision had not been easy, but it was a path I knew I had to walk.

One day, as I navigated my daily routine at the office, I overheard a hushed conversation that caught my attention. A few people were discussing Kaya and me. Their words painted a picture of betrayal, suggesting Kaya may have already moved on with her life. The implication hung heavily in the air, indicating that she had found someone else, someone they deemed more handsome and desirable. It was a conversation I couldn't escape, even if I wanted to.

My initial instinct was to pretend not to hear, to turn a deaf ear to the hurtful insinuations. But it was hard not to feel the weight of those words as they chipped away at my emotional armor. Over one and a half years, I had been exposed to countless such remarks, each a fresh jab at my heart.

The pain of hearing those whispers, of grappling with the possibility that Kaya had indeed moved on, was a struggle I couldn't hide. It was a wound that refused to heal, a nagging uncertainty that had become a constant companion I had thought I had moved on, but the truth was, my heart still carried the weight of our past.

I had reached a point where the past and present collided in a sea of ambiguity and uncertainty. The weight of the unspoken, the mystery surrounding Kaya's actions and the rumors that swirled around me were all threads woven into the fabric of a story far from over.

Time had passed quickly and over two years had slipped away without a word from Kaya. And in those silent years, much had changed in my life. I was no longer the team leader at the office; instead, my anger, loneliness and the gaping hole Kaya's absence left in my heart had transformed into an insatiable drive to throw myself into my work. The force propelled me forward, resulting in a promotion to the Manager position. People around me praised my resilience, hailing my transformation as if I had risen from the ashes, reborn like a phoenix. As long as I was working, keeping my mind occupied and my heart at bay, I could almost convince myself that I was back to being "normal."

My phone rang one afternoon amid the daily grind at the office. It was Vijay and he sounded excited, his voice brimming with anticipation. However, he didn't provide any immediate explanation for his enthusiasm. He urged me to meet him at a mall in the city, insisting that it was something I couldn't miss. Vijay had been dating a girl for over six months and the thought of him proposing to his girlfriend and she accepting his proposal filled my heart with joy. If that was the case, I didn't want to ruin his excitement by sharing the news with me instead of asking him if he had proposed to his girlfriend. Almost everyone our age in the office and families was either married or planning to marry soon. My family annoyed me with their nagging to find a girl and get married, but I avoided those discussions completely. Building a good career and name for myself has become my priority.

After ten minutes of his persistent pleas, I agreed to meet him at the mall. I wanted to hear some good news and his excitement gave me hope. When I left the office, it was already 6:50 in the evening. The drive from my office to the mall took approximately 25 minutes, a distance of just 10 kilometers. Unfortunately, during the dreaded peak traffic hours, the city's streets were choked with people leaving work and heading home. The slow-moving traffic reminded me of the ceaseless rhythm of life, each vehicle representing countless stories and I was just another passerby in this bustling urban symphony.

I navigated the maze of the mall's underground parking lot, finally finding a suitable spot to park my car. With a purpose, I approached the nearest lift, my anticipation building as I approached my rendezvous with Vijay. I decided to call him to coordinate our meeting, but the frustratingly poor mobile coverage thwarted my attempts. Frustration grew as I felt disconnected from his voice and his persistent actions wore my patience thin.

I decided to step out of the lift on the mall's ground floor, hoping for a better signal to reach Vijay. While on the ground floor, I dialed his number again, determined to get in touch. As the call connected, I couldn't hide my irritation and demanded his whereabouts. But all I could discern on the other end was a cacophony of honking horns and traffic noise, making any meaningful conversation impossible. It was frustrating to exchange garbled words; neither could comprehend the other.

I thought about messaging him rather than calling. I started typing the message and received an SMS from Vijay, providing a new location. He asked me to step outside the mall and cross the road, where he was waiting for me on the other side. It was a relief to have a clear direction and I wasted no time following his instructions. I anxiously crossed the bustling road, navigating the sea of vehicles and pedestrians and finally met Vijay on the opposite sidewalk. He was truly a pain in the butt that evening.

As I crossed the bustling road to meet Vijay on the opposite sidewalk, I couldn't help but feel a mix of curiosity and annoyance. I wondered why this game of cat and mouse was in the middle of the road. The question was burning on my lips and I wasted no time asking Vijay.

In response, Vijay casually brushed his phone against my face and I noticed that he had a picture displayed on the screen. My initial irritation shifted to confusion as I stared at the picture of shops inside the mall. I couldn't fathom why he was bugging me with a picture of the mall.

Before I could voice my exasperation, Vijay calmly instructed me to look at the photo closely. I focused on the picture, searching for hidden details that had eluded me. And then, it hit me like a bolt of lightning. There was a name on one of the store's boards in the notion whose name resembled someone I knew. I took a closer look and that name read Kaya.

It was all confusing why he showed me her name's picture.

I couldn't stop myself. "So what?" I asked Vijay with anger.

"It is her father's new shop; they opened this new store just a few weeks back," Vijay replied.

The shock washed over me like a tidal wave, leaving me speechless. Vijay's childlike behavior had cut through the years of silence and uncertainty, reminding me of a name that had once held a special place in my heart. Kaya's face had reemerged from the depths of my past, a beacon of hope and mystery that I thought I had left behind. The whirlwind of emotions that had settled during my time without her was reignited and I knew my journey was far from over.

"I am here because I saw Kaya going this way with her father," he added.

I jumped and hugged him in the middle of the road. Passers-by saw us laughing and acting like the kids we were at that moment.

A Forced Kiss

When I saw her name and learned about her family's whereabouts, ineffable happiness washed over me; it had been an eternity since I felt such genuine joy. Even though it offered only a vague glimpse of Kaya, that single photo had now become a cherished possession, second only to the memory of our first kiss in the office pantry. That moment was etched in my heart as the beginning of something profound. I couldn't envision anything surpassing its significance.

Reflecting on this newfound source of happiness, I realized I was reclaiming parts of my old self buried beneath the weight of silence and uncertainty. My family and friends sensed this transformation, even if they hadn't immediately voiced it. It was as if the air around me had lightened and the people I cared about most could detect my personality's subtle but profound shift.

Though I wasn't yet entirely the person I once was, I was getting closer to that familiar version of myself, one who could experience happiness, share laughter and relish life's simple pleasures. With the spark rekindled by the mere mention of Kaya, I was determined to explore the path ahead. I hoped it would lead me back to the world of emotions, connections and Kaya herself.

After years of yearning, I was finally ready to take the first step towards reuniting with Kaya. My heart pounded with a mixture of excitement and fear as I contemplated the journey that lay ahead. I knew that I needed to be patient and understanding. The loss of Kaya's younger sister had undoubtedly left a deep wound in her family's heart. I was determined to offer my support and comfort whenever I could. I wanted to be a source of strength and comfort during their grief.

I also yearned to meet Kaya's father and express my sincere love and admiration for Kaya. I understood that it might not be easy for an outsider to appear and claim a place in their family suddenly. However, I was determined to prove my worth. I was prepared to face any challenges that came my way and I was committed to seeing my pursuit of Kaya through to the end. My determination was fueled by my unwavering belief that Kaya and I were meant to be together. I knew our connection was genuine and our love was strong enough to overcome any obstacle. I was confident that I could earn the trust and respect of Kaya's family and I was eager to prove that I was worthy to marry Kaya.

As I embarked on the journey to win back Kaya's heart, I knew that the road ahead would not be easy. There would be moments of doubt and uncertainty. Sometimes, I would question my sanity for pursuing an unattainable love. But I was determined to succeed. I was confident that my passion for Kaya would guide me through the darkness.

I could not force Kaya to love me back, but I also knew I could not give up on her that easily. I would continue showing her my love and affection, hoping she would one day see me as the man I was. My journey was a testament to the power of love. It was a journey of hope, resilience and unwavering determination. It was a journey that would test the limits of my heart and soul. But I was prepared to face any challenge, for I knew that the reward at the end was worth any price. The question of how to contact Kaya's family and father still weighed heavily on my mind. I knew that I couldn't just show up at their doorstep unannounced. It would be disrespectful and intrusive.

I reached out to Anjali again, hoping she would reconsider her decision to help me. But she was adamant. She had no idea that Kaya and her family were back in Ahmedabad and she didn't want to get involved.

"I'm sorry, but I can't help you," she said. "I don't want to betray Kaya's trust."

I was disappointed, but I understood her position. Anjali had always been a loyal friend and I knew she wouldn't do anything she thought would hurt Kaya.

That weekend, Anjali visited Kaya's home. She finally met Kaya's mother, who told her that Kaya had started working again, helping her father at the store. Every day, she would go with her father and come back with him only, so meeting her while she was at the mall was nearly impossible.

I was starting to feel hopeless. I didn't know how I would ever get in touch with Kaya.

I talked with Payal and Vijay in the office, hoping they could help me. I hesitated to ask for their help, knowing I was putting them in a difficult position. But they were both willing to do whatever they could. Payal agreed to go to the mall and see if she could meet Kaya in person. She knew it would be a long shot but was willing to try.

Payal and her husband Sumit went to the mall the next weekend. They were able to find the store from the photo that I had given them.

Kaya was helping some other customers with their outfits. At first glance, everything looked normal to Payal. Kaya was acting completely normal like any other day you could imagine her to be.

After helping the others shop, Kaya approached Sumit and asked if she could show them some dresses. Payal seized the opportunity.

"Hi, Kaya, do you remember me?" she asked. "Payal from your office."

Kaya was shocked initially, but she quickly regained her composure.

"Of course, I remember you, Payal," she said. "How could I forget a strong female personality like you?"

Payal and Kaya talked briefly about work and old times. Then, Payal suggested that they step outside for a coffee.

Kaya asked her father for permission to step out for an hour or so. Her father knew that Kaya would be with another woman, so he gave her permission without hesitation.

Payal, Sumit and Kaya settled into a cozy corner of the coffee shop. They ordered tea and coffee and for a while, they chatted casually about their new store, the business and what Kaya had been up to. Kaya was curious about Payal's marriage and how everyone was doing at the office. Payal filled her in on the latest news and they laughed and reminisced about old times.

After a few minutes, Payal glanced at Sumit. "Would you mind taking a detour?" she asked. "I'd like to talk to Kaya in private."

Sumit nodded understandingly and stood up. "I'll be back in a bit," he said.

As soon as Sumit was out of earshot, Payal turned to Kaya and said, "If you don’t mind me asking, can I ask what happened with your sister and your family?"

Kaya's eyes welled up with tears. Payal reached out and offered her a tissue.

"It's okay," she said gently. "You don't have to talk about it if you don't want to."

But Kaya shook her head. "I want to," she said. "I just... I don’t know if I should burden you with my issues."

Kaya poured her heart out to Payal. She told her about her sister's death, the grief that had consumed her family and the struggles they had faced in the aftermath. She also revealed a secret about herself that almost destroyed her family emotionally.

Payal listened intently, offering words of comfort and support. Kaya's courage and resilience moved her.

When Kaya was finished speaking, she looked at Payal with pleading eyes. "Please don't tell anyone else about this," she said. "Not even Sumit." Kaya was unaware of why Payal was there; she had thought that Payal and Sumit were there for shopping and meeting her at the shop was just a coincidence.

Payal nodded. "Of course not," she said. "Your secret is safe with me."

By the time Sumit returned, Payal and Kaya were wiping away tears. "Everything okay?" he asked.

Payal smiled. "Yes, everything's fine," she said. "We were just having a girl talk."

Sumit bought a water bottle for the ladies and sat down beside Payal.

"So, Kaya," he said. "Have you talked to...?"

He trailed off, unable to bring himself to say my name.

Kaya shook her head. "No," she said. "I haven't."

Payal could see the pain in Kaya's eyes. She knew Kaya still had feelings for me, but she was resolved to move on with her life.

"I am trying to move on," Kaya said. "I have no place for anyone in my life right now. I must focus on my family and my father's new store."

Payal nodded. "I understand," she said; she couldn't help but wonder if Kaya was being honest with herself.

Payal reached out and took Kaya's hand. "Do you still have feelings for him?" she asked gently.

Kaya's eyes again welled up with tears; she didn't answer Payal's question.

"Why don't you reach out to him?" Payal added.

Kaya shook her head. "I can't," she said. "I shouldn't rob him of his happiness. He deserves to be with someone who can make him happy and proud. With me, he will not be able to live the life he deserves."

Payal couldn't argue with that; she knew that Kaya was right, but she also knew that Kaya was sacrificing her happiness for the sake of others. They finished their tea, returned to the store and shopped.

As they prepared to leave, Payal turned to Kaya and said, "Can I have your phone number? I'd love to keep in touch."

Kaya hesitated for a moment. "It's my old number," she said. "I don't keep it with me anymore and I haven't turned on my phone in ages."

"That's okay," Payal said. "I'll just text you and see if you get it."

Kaya nodded and recited her number. Payal entered it into her phone and sent a quick message. They said their goodbyes and Payal and Sumit walked away. As they walked, Sumit couldn't help but ask what the two of them talked about.

Payal hesitated. She didn't want to betray Kaya's trust. But she also knew she couldn't keep the truth from her husband. She was thinking deeply for a moment and decided to share only what she thought her husband should know—keeping Kaya's past secret.

"Kaya told me about her sister's death," she said. "And the pain her family has been through."

Sumit nodded. "That must have been difficult for her," he said.

"It was," Payal said. "And it's still affecting her. She is blaming herself somehow, stopping her from living her life."

Sumit looked at Payal concernedly. "What do you mean?" he asked.

Payal took a deep breath. "Kaya still loves him," she said.

Sumit was silent for a moment. Then, he said, "I know."

Payal looked at him in surprise. "How did you know?" she asked.

Sumit smiled. "It was obvious in the way she talked about him," he said. "How her eyes lit up when you asked her about him and when she spoke of his name."

Payal sighed. "I'm worried about her," she said. "She's putting on a brave face, but I can see she's hurting."

Sumit put his arm around Payal. "She'll be okay," he said. "She's a strong girl."

Payal nodded, but she wasn't so sure. She knew that Kaya was hurting and she knew that she was determined to keep her distance from me. As they drove home, Payal couldn't shake the feeling that Kaya was making a mistake. She knew that Kaya loved me and that I loved Kaya. But she also knew that Kaya was determined to keep her heart closed.

The next day, Payal received a text message from Kaya.

"I got your message," Kaya wrote. "I'll text him when I'm ready."

Payal smiled. It was a small start, but it was a start. She knew it would take time, but she was hopeful that Kaya would be able to open her heart again one day.

The next day, I met Payal for lunch. I was eager to hear what she had learned from Kaya.

"So, what did she say?" I asked.

Payal sighed. "It's not good," she said. "Kaya is still hurting. She's coping with her pain all alone."

"Does she still love me?" I asked.

Payal hesitated. "She didn't say that she didn't love you," she said. "But she did say that she wants to move on with her life."

"What does that mean?" I asked.

"I don't know," Payal said. "But I think it means she doesn't want to see you again."

I felt a wave of despair wash over me. I had been so hopeful that Kaya would be willing to give me another chance. But now, it seemed that my hopes were in vain.

"What should I do?" I asked.

Payal looked at me thoughtfully. "I think you should continue to pursue her," she said. "Be bolder and more aggressive with your approach."

"Why?" I asked. "If she doesn't want to see me, why should I keep trying?"

Payal smiled. "Because I believe you two are meant to be together," she said. "And I don't think Kaya is ready to give up on you yet."

Her words gave me a glimmer of hope. Maybe Kaya wasn't as closed off as I thought she was. She may need more time to heal.

"I'll do whatever it takes," I said. "I won't give up on Kaya."

Payal smiled. "I know you won't," she said. "And I'll be here to support you every step of the way."

Hearing Payal's positive words was a great feeling. It was reassuring to have someone who knew about our past and was rooting for my imagined happy future with Kaya.

I knew that it would be a long and difficult road ahead. But I was determined to win Kaya back. I would not give up on her.

Days turned into weeks and I dedicated myself to learning Kaya's routine. I observed her movements, noting the times she arrived at her father's store and the times she returned home.

I went back to my old routine. Every morning, I sent her a good morning message and every night, a goodnight. I didn't expect a response; I knew she was still hurting and didn't want to pressure her. I hoped that one day, she would read my messages and find the strength to reply.

I understood that Payal was right; Kaya still had feelings for me. I could imagine how she could have talked about me and how her eyes could have lit up when she spoke of my name. I also knew that she regretted not contacting me. She regretted breaking our promises and she was afraid; she was scared of getting hurt again. I understood her fear, but I also knew that I couldn't give up on her. I would continue to send her messages showing my love and affection for her. I hoped she would be ready to let me back into her life. In the meantime, I would focus on being the best man I could be. I would focus on making myself worthy of her love.

It would take time, so I was patient and willing to wait for her however long.

My behavior in the past year or so has been a source of concern for my family. They knew that something was troubling me, but I had refused to open up to them. They had asked me if there was someone I liked, but I had always denied it. I wasn't sure if I would ever see Kaya again and I didn't want to give them false hope. One weekend, during dinner, I asked my family if they wanted to go shopping and dinner.

"We just went shopping last week," my mother said. "We don't need anything."

Even though I wanted to see Kaya, I couldn’t force them to go shopping with me. I had denied their countless requests, so it was fair for them to deny my sudden request. After dinner, I was getting ready to go to my room when my mother called me into the living room.

"We need to talk," she said.

I sat down on the couch across from her. "What is it?" I asked.

"We've been worried about you," she said. "You've been so withdrawn lately. We know something is bothering you, but you won't tell us what it is."

I looked down at my mobile. "There is nothing you need to worry about," I said.

My mother reached out and took my mobile. "We're here for you," she said. "Whenever you're ready to talk, we'll listen."

I nodded. "Thank you," I said.

"In the meantime, we've decided it's time for you to start thinking about your future. We've been talking to some families and found a few girls who we think would be a good match for you." She said,

I felt a wave of panic wash over me. "I don't want to get married," I said.

My mother smiled. "Of course, you do," she said. "Every man wants to get married and create a family of his own."

"Not me," I said. "I'm not interested in getting married."

My mother's smile faded. "You're just saying that," she said. "You'll change your mind when you meet the right person."

"I'm not going to change my mind," I said. "I don't want to get married."

My mother stood up and shouted. "We'll talk about this later, but you need to start thinking about your future."

I watched as my mother walked out of the living room. I knew she wouldn't give up trying to find me a wife, but I was also determined to resist her efforts. I wasn't ready to move on from Kaya or prepared to start a new life with someone else.

"If you come with me and meet this girl and her family, I will go shopping with you," my mother said.

After a moment of deliberation, I agreed. The fact that I had been behaving more like my old self lately convinced them to come with me shopping. Whatever the reason, I was grateful for their willingness to accompany me. That weekend, we went to the mall. I was driving, so deciding where to go was up to me. I parked the car in the mall's basement and we began our shopping spree. After a while, my mother said she wanted to visit another store. She started walking in the direction of Kaya's store. I didn't say anything. This was why I had asked them to come shopping with me. I wanted to see Kaya.

I had thought that showing up alone might not go well with Kaya or her father, but I couldn't resist the urge to see her. My mother entered the store and Kaya immediately approached her. I stood outside the store, waiting for the rest of my family to enter. As they all went inside, I made my way toward my mother.

My eyes met Kaya's briefly, but she quickly looked away. I kept my eyes on her as she interacted with my mother. To me, she was still the most beautiful girl in the world. But something had changed in her. Her eyes were smaller than usual and the smile that could have melted anyone's heart was gone. The smile she offered to my mother wasn't the real one.

We spent nearly 30 minutes in the store, but Kaya avoided me the entire time. She acted like I was a stranger and our time together meant nothing to her. Her indifference hurt me, but I wasn't surprised. I knew that she was still hurting from her sister's death and somewhere deep inside her heart, she knew that she had done injustice to our relationship. I knew that she wasn't ready to face me yet. I wouldn't give up on her; I would wait for her for as long as it took and find a way to win her back. Before we could leave her store, I hoped for eye contact, but she was more determined in not looking at me than I had imagined.

After shopping and dinner that weekend, we returned home. We sat in the living room, discussing how good it had been to go shopping and have dinner as a family. My family spent a lot of time together, but one person was always missing from those gatherings: me. I had forced myself to work and avoid family gatherings as much as possible. Every gathering I had attended lately had ended with the same question: why wasn't I ready for a marriage? Did I like someone?

I wouldn't say I liked those questions. They made me feel like I was being judged. They made me feel like I failed to meet my family's expectations. Living in a joint family means delivering on your family's expectations and being compared to your cousins and distant families. I knew that my family just wanted what was best for me. They wanted me to be happy, but their constant pressure was frustrating. Sometimes, it felt like I was suffocating by their questions, so I stopped attending those family dinners and gatherings.

"Did you see that girl in the store?" my mother asked.

I looked at her in surprise. "What, girl?" I asked.

"The one you were staring at," she said. "The one you couldn't take your eyes off of."

I felt my cheeks flush with heat. "I wasn't staring at anyone," I said.

"Oh, really?" my mother said. "Then why didn't you answer me when I asked you for your opinion on the dresses I was buying?"

I didn't have an answer for that. I had lost my thoughts and hadn't even heard her ask me a question. "I knew that girl," I said. "She used to work in my office."

My mother's eyes lit up. "Oh, really?" she said. "What was her name?"

"Kaya," I replied.

My cousin broke a glass in the kitchen, which stopped the interrogation by my mother and I started walking towards my room. “I am going to bed; good night,” I said before entering my room. I closed the door behind me, sat on my bed and buried my face in my hands. I didn't know why Kaya would react that way; she did not even look at me once. I wanted to talk with her, watch her smile and listen to her voice. What happened at the mall was something other than what I had planned. I had hoped for a better outcome, at the very least, a casual hi or hello.

Trapped in a cycle of my own making, I had avoided my family and friends because I didn't want them asking me any questions, especially not about Kaya. Drowning in sorrow, I didn't know how long I could take it. With mixed emotions, I closed my eyes and drifted off to sleep, dreaming of a day when I could finally hold her in my arms again.

The next few weeks passed by rapidly. Per my daily routine, I send a good morning message to Kaya right after waking up and a good night text before bed. Then, I waited for her response for the rest of the day.

I had almost forgotten my promise to my family because I was too focused on Kaya. However, one afternoon, my mother stopped me while I was leaving for the office.

"Take next week off on Sunday; we will visit your uncle's home to meet a girl and her family." My mother told me.

I felt a wave of anger wash over me and said, "I don't want to see any girl right now. I'm not interested in getting married."

My mother looked at me sternly and said, "You made a promise and you're going to keep it."

I knew that there was no arguing with her. She was determined to find me a girl and wouldn't stop until she succeeded.

"Fine, I'll go," I said as I stormed out of the house and drove to the office. I was so angry that I could barely think straight.

I have had my fair share of meetings with girls and have become a pro when forcing girls to reject me. If nothing would work against my mother setting up these meetings, I always had that weapon in my arsenal, I thought and continued with my tiresome life.

As I reached the office, I called Vijay for a smoke. We met at the office terrace for a smoke before starting my day there. I was angry at my mother, but I was also grateful. It was because of her that I was able to see Kaya. Vijay knew just by looking at my face that I had another meaningless fight with someone in my family. I wasn't thinking about Kaya, only when I was working. Somehow, I found a moment of peace in my work.

A few days passed and that weekend morning, I was sleeping in my room when my mother abruptly entered my room and shattered the tranquility. It was around 10:00 a.m. and her nagging voice pierced through the layers of my sleep, urging me to wake up.

“Get up and, at the very least, trim your beard so you look like a decent guy and a member of this family,” she nagged.

I was angry to be woken up very early on a weekend morning. I protested by pulling the blanket over my head and asking, "Why are you being so annoying, especially at this time of day on the weekend?"

My mother was determined to keep her promise and reminded me that we had agreed to visit my uncle's house that day. She explained that it had been difficult to find a time that worked for everyone and now that we had settled on a date, it was important to follow through.

"Get out of bed now," she said with anger.

As soon as my mother mentioned the words "uncle" and "schedule," my heart sank. I knew what it meant - I would have to meet another potential girl. It was a recurring event that always filled me with anxiety. Whenever my mother used these words, it was a signal that I would be taken to some relative's or stranger's house to go through the nerve-wracking process of meeting a potential match.

Despite resisting such arrangements, I always ended up on the losing side. Whether it was a one-on-one argument with my family members or a collective action where I was hopelessly outnumbered, I never won.

Despite my unwillingness, it was clear that I had no choice but to accept my fate. So, I reluctantly peeled myself out of bed and headed to the salon to trim my beard as requested by my mother. However, as I sat in the chair, I felt a spirit of rebellion coursing through my veins. In a quiet act of defiance, I boldly decided to go further and opt for a clean shave. Even though I knew I was still bound for the looming meeting, this act of rebellion was my way of subtly disregarding my family's expectations. I had to attend the event, looking dramatically different from what they had anticipated.

After leaving the salon, I felt like a completely different person. My face, previously covered in facial hair, was now smooth and clean. When I returned home, I greeted my family with a slightly mocking smile as if challenging them to say something about my sudden change in appearance. To my amusement, they didn't say anything and seemed to have accepted that I would do something unpredictable.

Everyone sat in their cars while grinding their teeth; I followed suit and got into a car with my cousins. As I got into the car with my cousins, I felt the weight of the upcoming meeting on my shoulders. It was a familiar situation where societal norms clashed with my personal preferences. I knew I had to follow the plan, but I was resolved not to give up easily. As we started our journey, my mind was in a whirlwind of plotting and strategizing, preparing for the storm about to hit my family.

The drive to my relative's house took about half an hour. As we pulled up, I felt anxiety tightening in my stomach. I knew I was about to meet another girl my family had chosen for me. I had to act polite and charming, even though I was not interested in getting married. I went upstairs with my cousins and waited for the girls' family to arrive. We sat there talking about all the other girls I had met and how they had all rejected me. My cousins discussed and analyzed the reasons for rejections, trying to figure out what I was doing wrong.

My phone rang. It was my father. "Come downstairs," he said. "The family is almost here. They're parking their car outside."

I went downstairs with my cousin and we sat on the side of the living room, keeping a place for another family to sit. I was scrolling through my Facebook feed when the other family arrived. My family exchanged greetings with them as they settled into their seats. My aunt, who knew the girl's family, instructed the girl to sit right in front of me.

"Kaya, come sit here, beta," she said.

I lost my grip on my phone as I heard the name. My eyes darted around the room, searching for her. She was sitting there, right in front of me. It was Kaya.

I couldn't believe it. I had never expected to see her again. Kaya sat across from me with an elegant posture that showed her strength. She wore a simple, contemporary, soft blue outfit that complemented her slim figure. Her brown eyes, usually lively and bright, now seemed tinged with sadness. Her hair, usually a wild cascade, was tied back in a loose ponytail today. Strands of hair framed her face and the light from the window gave it a beautiful glow. Although she looked tired, she still had a resilient gaze that reflected her strong character. Kaya's outfit blended traditional elegance with modern style. She wore a black bindi on her forehead, which added to her classic look.

As she sat there, she looked nervous. Occasionally, her fingers were entwined and tapped to the rhythm of her thoughts. Her earrings swayed slightly with the movement. Despite the sadness that seemed to envelop her, there was an undeniable aura of self-reliance and inner strength about her. In that moment, Kaya was a reminder of the complexity of the human soul.

As I stared at her, I hoped to make eye contact. I was transported back to a time when our hearts beat as one. I remembered the way she would laugh, the way she would touch me, the way she would look at me with those captivating eyes. She did not look at me; she held her head down and sat there.

I looked at my aunt. "Can I talk to her alone?" I asked.

Hearing my voice, Kaya looked at me and was also in shock. We had no idea how our families knew each other and who arranged this meeting at my uncle's home. Kaya and everyone else, including Kaya's parents, looked at me as if I had asked something outrageous.

"Please," I added while looking at my father.

My aunt looked at my uncle and father. "Yes," she said. "Why not? That's the whole reason you're both here."

I excused myself and asked Kaya to follow me to my cousin's room. I closed the door behind me as soon as Kaya entered.

A million questions were swirling around in my head, my heart was pounding and my body temperature was rising. I grabbed her hand and led her to the bed. I pulled a chair up close to her and sat down. Mustering up my courage, I approached her. As I sat before her, I could feel my heart pounding.

“How are you, Kaya?” I asked, my voice barely a whisper.

After learning about her and her family, I sent her thousands of messages and called her hundreds of times. I thought she would reply, but she just sat there defying my expectations.

"You know I still love you, right?" I added, breaking the silence.

She kept looking down at her hands, her silence deafening.

"I did everything possible to contact you these past two years, but you never responded. Not even once. Why?" I questioned, my voice trembling with emotion.

"Why did you shut me out of your life? What did I do so wrong?" My voice trembled, barely concealing the turmoil beneath. As I struggled to maintain my composure, my eyes betrayed me, brimming with unshed tears. A single tear escaped, tracing a silent path down my cheek, ending in a quiet splash against my wrist.

She sat across from me, still and quiet, her head bowed. Tears rolled down her cheeks, showing our unspoken feelings and thoughts. Her silence was deep and sad, more than words could ever say.

"What can I do to go back to how we were? Was it your father or something that happened with your sister?" I added after wiping my eyes.

"Tell me something, Kaya," I asked again with frustration.

My eyes pleaded for an answer, any sign that she still cared. Tears trickled down her cheeks as she lifted her head to meet my gaze.

"I'm so sorry," she said, her voice choking with tears. "I'm so sorry I couldn't reply to your messages and phone calls and I am sorry for disappearing without saying anything."

She looked down at her hands again, her fingers fidgeting nervously.

Kaya's eyes glistened with unshed tears as they threatened to spill over. Her emotional turmoil was palpable, like a storm brewing beneath her surface. I couldn't stand by and watch her suffer any longer. I gently took her trembling hand without hesitation, pulling her closer.

For a moment, Kaya remained stiff in my arms, her body seemingly frozen by the weight of her emotions. Then, the dam burst and her cries poured forth. The first sobs were hushed, like a gentle rain, but they soon crescendoed into a torrential downpour of grief. I held her tightly, attempting to offer solace in the face of her anguish. As her cries echoed through the room, I whispered words of consolation into her ear, a desperate attempt to alleviate her suffering.

I apologized for her pain, acknowledging that words could never truly mend what had been broken. I vowed to always be there for her, no matter the circumstances. Slowly but surely, her sobs began to subside and the tension in her body began to ease. She leaned into my embrace, seeking comfort and refuge, the tears slowly ceasing.

We stood embraced in the quiet, the weight of unspoken questions and echoes of our shared past hanging in the air. The reality of what was once an impossible dream settled over us and the gravity of the moment was palpable.

After a brief, contemplative silence, Kaya delicately moved her hands, silently asking for a moment of space. Yet, I couldn't bring myself to let her go just yet. Before she could untangle herself, I leaned in, capturing her lips with mine.

At first, Kaya resisted, attempting to break the kiss. However, I was resolute, gently but firmly persevering until her struggles began to fade. Gradually, she surrendered to the intoxicating intensity of the kiss, her hands clutching my shirt, pulling me closer.

Our kiss was a culmination of years of longing, passion and desire. It was a vibrant, desperate and tender exchange that bridged the chasm of our separation. Each moment apart had led us to this point, where our hunger for each other was undeniable.

When we finally pulled away, both of us were left breathless, our hearts racing. Our eyes met, reflecting an insatiable yearning and unspoken promises. In that singular instant, the weight of the past seemed inconsequential. All that mattered was our reunion and the profound understanding that our bond was unbreakable.

For the next few minutes, we sat together, a mixture of tears and laughter punctuating the overwhelming emotions that enveloped us.

Contradiction

In the wake of our unexpected reunion, we went downstairs into the familial gathering. The room was abuzz with curious relatives and our families, eager to learn the fate of Kaya's decision regarding our connection. As we found our seats, the questions began rolling in like a ceaseless curiosity. They wanted to know if Kaya would follow suit, rejecting me as countless other girls had done.

The teasing commenced, light and playful, but it was enough to coax a blush from Kaya's cheeks. She endured the playful jabs with grace and a hint of embarrassment, her eyes casting fleeting glances in my direction. We had once been so close; now, we were two worlds apart, both haunted by our shared past.

As time flowed on, my aunt, the matron of the gathering, called me to the forefront of this familial quest. It was my turn to be examined and stand beneath the scrutiny of Kaya's family. My heart raced with anticipation, anxiety and a tinge of excitement. I knew that I had to face this interrogation with confidence and charm.

Aunt's request was straightforward and her eyes sparkled with curiosity. "Introduce yourself to Kaya's family," she said, a knowing smile dancing on her lips.

I looked around at the assembled group, bracing for the volley of questions. Yet, before anyone could utter a word, I held up my hand, effectively halting the oncoming storm of inquiries. The room fell silent and all eyes turned to me.

"What would you like to know about me?" I inquired, my voice calm but filled with the assurance that I had something important to say. The room waited in expectant silence, each individual intrigued by my confidence. Before anyone could ask, I continued, my eyes never leaving Kaya's father, who sat at the group's center.

"Allow me to save you the trouble of questions," I declared, my tone resonant with conviction. "I am the one person in this room who can rightfully claim to be the perfect match for Kaya." My gaze remained steady, locking onto Kaya's father. I sensed the weight of his expectations and his protective demeanor.

"I promise I will do everything within my power to ensure that Kaya feels safe, cherished and content," I pledged, my words carrying the weight of sincerity. "In pursuing her happiness, I will be her unwavering support, the anchor she can always rely on."

A sense of determination coursed through my veins as I addressed Kaya's family. At that moment, I was making a promise, not only to them but to Kaya herself. The room was still, but I could see understanding dawning in their eyes. I knew that actions would always speak louder than words, but these words were a start, a testament to my unwavering commitment to Kaya and a declaration of my intention to rewrite our shared history.

As the evening unfolded, my ever-inquisitive cousins couldn't resist delving into the intricacies of our relationship. Eager to satisfy their curiosity, I decided to share the essence of our story, ensuring I didn't inadvertently cast shadows on Kaya and her family.

With a lighthearted smile, I began recounting our tale, blending nostalgia with the excitement of our present encounter. I described our first meeting in the office, the fortunate encounter that seemed distant yet fresh in my memory. The narrative flowed, painting a picture of our journey from acquaintances to close friends and then to a relationship. I omitted moments of heartache and longing, choosing to focus on the enduring bond that brought us to this moment.

My feelings for Kaya were evident in every word and every story shared. I couldn't conceal the fondness and admiration I held for her. Kaya sat beside me, a silent observer of my narrative, occasionally casting fleeting glances my way. Despite her reserved demeanor, it was clear that my words hadn't fallen on deaf ears. Her gaze, a silent acknowledgment, spoke volumes about her feelings.

Throughout the conversations, Kaya remained in her realm, speaking only when compelled, with responses often limited to 'yes' and 'no.' Her silence, discomfiting to some, was not lost on me. I understood that beneath her reserved exterior lay a treasure trove of unspoken, complex emotions—a puzzle waiting to be unraveled.

As the evening wore on and the room bathed in warm, golden light, the whirlwind of emotions seemed to dance around us. The families engaged in polite discourse, sharing stories, laughter and occasional banter. Each moment added another thread to the intricate tapestry of our union, revealing the gathering's significance beyond mere formality.

Finally, as the evening drew to a close, Kaya and her family decided it was time to leave. The farewell involved formalities, well-wishing and promises of future meetings. The atmosphere carried a blend of hope, expectation and a touch of nostalgia. The unspoken understanding connected us all like a delicate thread.

As their departure neared, an urgency surged within me. My desire to speak with Kaya privately, ensuring her safety and continuing our conversation, was unmistakable. Turning to her with genuine concern, I requested something that felt like a lifeline.

"Kaya, please do me a favor," I implored, locking my gaze on hers. "Send me a message once you reach home. I can call you later and we can continue our talk."

Kaya responded with a subtle nod and a faint but reassuring smile. It was a promise, an unspoken pact between us. As her family prepared to depart and the formalities drew close, I couldn't help but hold onto that promise like a lifeline. Our journey had begun anew and it was a path I was determined to walk with her, step by step, no matter where it led.

With the departure of Kaya's family, our home transformed into a sanctuary of whispers and contemplation. Both families assembled in the living room, their voices a soft murmur as they discussed and mapped out the future steps ahead. The air was imbued with purpose and anticipation as if we were all aware that something momentous was afoot.

Sitting among our families, I couldn't resist asking my mother - my closest confidant - a question that had puzzled me for a while. "How did you know, Mother? How could you see my love for Kaya, the feelings I had concealed for a long time?"

My cousin revealed a story that was important to me. It was about Vijay's visit, a part of our lives that I didn't know about. Vijay was a trusted friend who delivered a message that would change my life. He spoke passionately about my love for Kaya and convinced my family that I was a man of unwavering devotion. He assured them that my heart belonged only to Kaya and would never be swayed by anyone else.

My cousin shared this story with me and it was a secret kept hidden from me until that day. The emotions I had kept hidden, the passion I had concealed, were now exposed for everyone to see. I felt both vulnerable and liberated at the same time.

As soon as I revealed my feelings for Kaya, my family members exchanged knowing glances and suddenly, everything became clear. The affection I had kept to myself for so long was now shared among us all as if a bridge had been constructed connecting my heart to theirs. This bridge was built upon the pillars of Vijay's conviction as a true friend and my unwavering devotion to Kaya.

As the evening progressed, the room was filled with emotions, unity and hope for a better future. Amidst all the discussions and exchange of plans, I eagerly awaited a message. Finally, as the night drew its velvet curtain across the sky, my phone vibrated gently. It was a message from Kaya, a testament to her feelings and a symbol of her need for privacy. I read her message with bated breath. It was a soft announcement that they had arrived home safely. Her simple yet significant gesture proved that our connection was not limited to physical presence. It assured me she was always a message away and our conversation could continue without hindrance. This promise warmed my heart and filled me with joy.

I was eager to hear her voice again and couldn't resist responding. I asked if she was alone and if we could talk more, but her response was delivered with gentle consideration and veiled in her natural politeness. She indicated that the night had taken its toll on her and she wished for a moment's respite to reconnect with her family and enjoy a peaceful night's rest. She requested that we wait until morning to continue our conversation.

I wanted to talk with her for some more time, but I knew patience and giving her the time she needed was important. As the night went on, new secrets would be revealed and the dawn would bring new opportunities. The clock kept ticking away and with the promise of a new day on the horizon, our story of conflicting emotions and enduring love would continue to unfold.

The next morning, as our family gathered around the dining table, I couldn't help but ask my mother a question that had been on my mind since the previous evening. "When should we invite Kaya and her family to our home?" I inquired with a mix of excitement and anticipation.

My question elicited laughter from my family and they wasted no time seizing the opportunity to tease me. Amidst their laughter, my mother chimed in, her amusement palpable. "You, my dear," she said, "were not so eager to marry just any girl."

The rest of my family members joined in the laughter, their joy infectious and I couldn't help but chuckle along with them. It was, after all, a testament to the profound event that had occurred in my life.

My father, always the voice of reason and wisdom in our household, calmly mentioned that arranging the meetings with Kaya's family would require a few days. He explained that my uncle, responsible for coordinating these significant events, had been called away on urgent business, adding complexity to the planning.

However, I felt rather audacious at that moment, a boldness fueled by my newfound resolve and the certainty that Kaya and I were meant to be together. I shamelessly implored them to expedite the process to make our intentions official without delay. In that instant, I was walking on the moon, the proverbial head in the clouds.

Determined to see this plan through, later that day, I made a phone call to Kaya, a call that was not without its share of nervous anticipation. "Would you like to have dinner with me?" I asked, my voice steady despite the butterflies in my stomach.

Kaya's reply was considerate, hinting at her respect for her father's wishes. She explained that she would need to seek her father's permission. I turned to my mother with a request of my own; I asked if she would reach out to Kaya's mother and seek her approval for our dinner date.

Standing by my mother's side, I watched as she dialed Kaya's mother's number, a tangible connection between our families and our intentions. When Kaya's mother answered, my mother, with utmost grace, requested her permission. However, she learned that only Kaya's father held the authority to grant such permissions. Kaya's mother promised to speak with him regarding our proposal.

I had to keep going with my day, so I went to work. My mind was racing with thoughts and my heart was beating fast with excitement while I waited for Kaya's response. It felt like time was standing still as I waited. Finally, as the day turned into evening, Kaya messaged me back. She said that we couldn't have dinner together, but her father had permitted us to meet up for coffee at the mall.

I suggested meeting at a coffee shop in the mall at 7:30 that evening. Excited to see her, I left work and asked my colleague Vijay to take care of everything in the office. He knew where my heart was leading me and agreed to help. However, I got stuck in traffic on the way and was delayed. I thought maybe a motorcycle would have been faster, but it was too late for that now. Every red light and congested road seemed to slow me down.

When I reached the mall and managed to secure a parking spot, time slipped through my fingers like grains of sand. It was already 7:50 and my heart raced with expectation and guilt. Hurrying into the coffee shop, I found Kaya waiting for me, her presence a soothing balm for my anxiety.

Our eyes met and I couldn't help but apologize for my tardiness. "I'm so sorry for being late," I confessed with genuine remorse, my voice carrying the weight of my apologies.

Kaya's response was gracious, as she comforted me and acknowledged the unpredictable nature of city traffic. She had already ordered tea for me, a gesture that warmed my heart. Expressing my gratitude, I took her hand and gently kissed them.

Her reaction, however, was unexpected. She withdrew her hand and began to survey the surroundings, nervous tension in her demeanor. "What are you looking for?" I inquired, unable to suppress my curiosity.

She leaned closer, her words a hushed whisper. "Most of these store owners know my father," she confided, a reminder of the constraints placed upon her by her family's reputation.

We settled into conversation, with my words flowing freely and Kaya, for the most part, listening attentively. It felt like time stood still, as though the world had narrowed to just the two of us.

Kaya's phone rang and interrupted our conversations. She answered and it was her father on the other end. Kaya's face showed she felt bad leaving, but she had to return home with her father. Even though we lost track of time, she couldn't ignore her duty. Before going in a hurry, she promised to text me. As she left, I felt a sense of longing and anticipation.

As the days passed, I diligently adhered to my routine of sending a "good morning" message at the break of the day and a "good night" message before retiring to sleep. The distinction was that now, Kaya's replies punctuated each of my messages. It was a rhythm of communication that mirrored the growing connection between us, a promise of blossoming affection and the anticipation of shared moments yet to come.

The days that followed were a harmonious melody of happiness. I was content and my family was the happiest in my life then. Their joy stemmed from discovering why I had hesitated to consider marriage with anyone else. As I reflected on it, it became increasingly clear to me that their approval of Kaya, of all people, was nothing short of miraculous. My family was deeply rooted in our age-old traditions and it was an unexpected twist of fate to see them embrace my decision.

With each passing day, my heart swelled with anticipation as we awaited my uncle's return from his business trip. His return marked the key to arranging meetings and setting dates for our formal engagement, a moment of great significance in our journey together. The days flew by in a flurry of activity as my family and I immersed ourselves in the delightful hustle and bustle of shopping, selecting jewelry and picking out clothes for Kaya. It was a cherished tradition that added to the sense of jubilation in our household.

During this time, I received a tip from my cousin, who had been keeping close tabs on developments. My uncle had returned from his business trip, ready to engage with Kaya's family to coordinate the upcoming family gatherings. It was a significant step in bringing our families closer, aligning our destinies and formalizing the path ahead.

As I returned from the office one evening, I entered a somewhat unexpected scene. The clock's hands had moved well past midnight and the living room was still alive with conversation. My uncle and parents were engrossed in dialogue and as I stepped in, I offered my greetings, acknowledging my uncle's presence.

Tired from the day's work, I went to my room. "I'll be back in a minute," I mumbled to my family, indicating my intention to return shortly. I quickly freshened up, washing my face and slipping into comfortable nightwear. I returned to the family room a few minutes later, only to find my uncle had already left.

Curiosity compelled me to question my father, who was still there. I inquired about the nature of their late-night discussion.

His response was simple, "It got late, so he left." My energy reserves were running low and the lateness of the hour had begun to weigh on me, so I exchanged goodnight wishes with everyone and retreated to my room.

Before settling into bed, I couldn't resist sending Kaya a heartfelt message. It was a simple "good night" with a heart emoji, a small gesture that held the power to brighten the darkest of nights and whisper promises of the days to come.

As we sat down for breakfast as a family the next morning, an unusual silence fell over our typically lively conversations. The atmosphere felt unsettling as if something had shadowed our home.

The silence was too noticeable to ignore, so I interjected with a little humor, "What's happening? Has someone died?" I said this to ease the tension, but my mother didn't respond with laughter or reassurance that everything was okay. Instead, she got up from her chair and went to the kitchen without saying a word.

I felt increasingly confused as I turned to my father, who was sitting next to me. I couldn't help but ask him, "Papa, what's going on?" However, his response only added to my confusion. He calmly told me to finish my breakfast, avoiding my question altogether. This left me even more concerned and unsure about what was happening.

The atmosphere at the dining table was tense and an unusual silence hung heavy in the air despite everyone eating. An unspoken agreement had been reached and the meal continued without the usual conversation. The silence left an awkward feeling in the room. Once the plates were cleared and the meal had ended, I felt the need to confront my father again, unwilling to let this mystery continue. My father heaved a deep sigh before finally revealing the cause of the tension: "Kaya's family has rejected our request for a meeting."

The revelation I received was shocking and my mind struggled to comprehend its implications. I couldn't resist asking my father the reason behind it. I needed to understand why things had taken such an unexpected turn and his response would provide the key to unlocking the truth.

"I'm sorry, we don't have the answers," he said, his voice filled with disappointment. "Your uncle is currently working on getting more information from them." He got up from the table, leaving me with many unanswered questions that hung like an unsolved puzzle.

A mountain of rejection loomed before us, blocking what had initially appeared to be the start of a promising and joyous journey. I couldn't help but express my bewilderment and frustration, "I thought they liked me and everything was going great between me and Kaya." My feet carried me toward my father, seeking answers in the face of uncertainty.

"I know, beta," he replied with empathy, recognizing the disappointment etched on my face. "We'll have to wait for your uncle to find out why they decided." The prospect of waiting felt like an eternity and I was not ready to endure such uncertainty. My impatience led me to the car and I set off towards Kaya's father's store, hoping to meet him and demand an explanation.

However, my quest proved fruitless as I reached the store, only to discover Kaya and her father were absent. Feeling disheartened and seeking some explanation, I turned to the person behind the store counter. "Do you know where Kaya and her father are?" I inquired.

With a shrug, he responded, "They had somewhere to go, so I'm managing the store today. Every once in a while, they don't come to the store." His words left me even more perplexed and I headed back to my office with nowhere else to turn. The passing hours were laden with tension, my anticipation growing as I continually checked my phone, hoping for a response from

Kaya. The lack of replies left me restless and unable to concentrate on my work.

As night descended, the uncertainty weighed heavily on me. Instead of sending a customary goodnight message, I took a bolder step: I called Kaya. I tried to reach her through messages and calls, but the silence on the other end was deafening. Frustration mounted and as I lay in bed, I couldn't recall when sleep finally overtook me. Once filled with hope and happiness, my dreams had now turned into unsettling nightmares where my family, too, was engulfed in the shadows of uncertainty.

My family's vibrant, talkative members had fallen unnaturally quiet after this unexpected decision. It was a blow that shook the foundations of our familial unity as if someone had maliciously snatched away the little happiness we had managed to grasp onto. The echo of their rejection reverberated through our lives, leaving us with an overwhelming sense of emptiness.

My determination was noticeable the next afternoon as we gathered around the dining table for lunch. I looked at my mother and posed a question that had been burning within me, "I will meet Kaya's father and talk to him myself."

My mother, ever the voice of reason, responded after a contemplative glance at my father, "We should wait for a few more days, dear. What do you think?" She turned to my father, seeking his opinion.

My father, a steadfast figure in our family, offered his perspective, addressing me directly, "Yes, you should let us elders handle these things. We must exercise patience. More will be revealed in a few days." His gaze remained steady on me.

While their words of caution carried a weight of experience and tradition, they couldn't suppress the determination that had ignited within me. Though I didn't voice my disagreement, I had already decided to take matters into my own hands. Starting the very next day, I began visiting Kaya's home before heading to the office, hoping to encounter her father and finally gain some clarity on this perplexing situation.

Each morning, I stood patiently outside her apartment gate, longing for an opportunity to speak with her father. After three weeks of waiting, I finally managed to intercept him on his way to the apartment. I halted his progress without hesitating and inquired if I could speak with him. Despite his displeasure, he agreed to converse with me privately and invited me into their home.

Once inside, he offered me a glass of water and gestured for me to take a seat. However, the tension in the room was real as his disappointment in me became apparent. "Why are you creating a scene like a child?" He questioned with a heavy sigh. "You've grown up and should act like one."

His words did little to deter me. I interjected before he could continue, "What is wrong with me that you're denying our relationship and the possibility of marriage?" I questioned, my emotions surging forth. "I want to marry your daughter and I believe I possess all the qualities a father seeks in a son-in-law. It feels like you're depriving your daughter of her happiness. Have you ever asked Kaya what she truly wants?" My relentless questioning flowed without regard for his feelings, as I believed he intentionally blocked our path to happiness.

However, the truth was far more complex than I had realized. My barrage of questions ceased abruptly when I saw tears welling in his eyes. He replied, trembling, "You think I'm stopping her from marrying you."

Unable to hide my exasperation, I retorted, "If not you, then who else?" The puzzle of their sudden resistance baffled me.

Kaya's father responded with a profound sadness in his eyes, wiping away his tears, "It is Kaya's decision, not mine. I will not force her into a marriage if she doesn't want to." The weight of his words hung heavily in the air, carrying the gravity of an untold story.

This revelation left me in a state of profound confusion. I looked at him, asking, "What are you talking about? What has Kaya told you?"

He sighed and said, "I'm not sure you know everything about Kaya. Your colleague Payal knows about the whole story."

The weight of the truth was overwhelming, the secrets buried beneath the surface, ready to shatter the semblance of my world. Even after our profound connection, Kaya's inexplicable decision to withhold her heart from me had been a mystery that gnawed at me relentlessly. It had led me to confront her father and beseech him for an explanation, to understand what lay beneath Kaya's pain.

Kaya's decision, Payal knowing why Kaya did not want to marry me, was all confusing, I mused, grappling with the jigsaw puzzle of my life. Finally, I posed the question to Kaya's father, asking him to share everything with me from the beginning.

His response was cautious, his voice measured, as he inquired, "How much do you know?" I met his gaze with steely determination and replied, "Tell me everything from day one." The gravity of the situation and the sense of urgency compelled me to seek answers, no matter the cost.

With a heavy sigh, Kaya's father agreed to disclose the hidden story. He made it abundantly clear that our conversation must remain a well-guarded secret. He did not want Kaya to discover that he had unburdened his heart to me, leaving me the sole bearer of this hidden truth in my family. It was a promise I was willing to make for understanding and love.

We settled into a conversation that spanned several hours, during which Kaya's father recounted a harrowing narrative of his family's past. If words could encapsulate the pain, suffering, agony and anguish that had enveloped Kaya's family, they would not suffice. The hardships they had endured surpassed the limits of my imagination, painting a picture of despair that shook me to my core. Especially when he mentioned what transpired with Kaya and her sister. Kaya had experienced many losses and struggles throughout her journey, leaving deep emotional scars. Despite these challenges, she remained resilient and bravely faced life's difficulties. She carried heavy burdens, often beyond her age; she sometimes lost the hope and will to live.

Through the sad tales and heart-wrenching accounts, I began to fathom why Kaya's heart had become a fortress, sealed off from the world. Her experiences left indelible scars and unhealed wounds that no love could easily mend. I had met her under the guise of a fresh start, but I now understood that her past was intertwined with a legacy of torment that had left her beyond repair.

As I listened, my eyes welled up with tears and I felt a pain that transcended empathy. Kaya's father tried to hide his emotions, wiping away tears that stubbornly refused to cease. Now barely audible, his voice trembled as he confessed, "Now, you know everything there was to know."

He paused for a moment, his emotions betraying him. Then, sorrowfully, he continued, "If you still wish to marry my daughter, I will not create any hurdles. All I want for my daughter is to be happy." It was a gesture of selflessness, a plea for me to be the source of happiness in Kaya's life despite her staggering challenges.

I sat on the edge of my chair, my capacity for speech utterly abandoned. The pain in my chest was nearly unbearable and it felt as though my heart was being cruelly wrenched from my chest. The truths I had just learned were far beyond the boundaries of my darkest imaginings. I could not reconcile the vivacious, beautiful Kaya I had met with the suffering that now painted her family's past.

The hours passed in a daze, the weight of this newfound knowledge bearing down upon me. Finally, after an eternity, I rose from my seat and bid Kaya's father farewell, unable to fully express my emotions. My heart and mind were grappling with the magnitude of what I had just uncovered and the path ahead was anything but clear. As I left their home, I stopped my car near my home and stood there smoking and thinking of Kaya. I called her, but her mobile phone was switched off.

The next day, my mind was in chaos with numerous unanswered questions. I couldn't stop the continuous stream of thoughts that demanded answers. The overwhelming burden of knowledge, especially the reason behind Payal's silence, weighed heavily on me like a never-ending mountain. It felt as if I had been living in a world painted with half-truths and concealed realities and the only way out was to confront the painful secrets shrouded in the dark.

I dialed Payal's number with my resolve bolstered by a newfound determination. It was an anxious moment, a pivotal step towards understanding the enigma surrounding me. The one person I had always trusted to guide me was now at the center of my quest for truth.

Payal agreed to meet me at the office cafeteria. That day, when I reached the office, Payal and I met at the cafeteria and as we sat down, I felt a torrent of emotions surging within me. My heart was heavy and my eyes betrayed the turmoil beneath the surface.

"How could you not tell me?" I implored, locking my gaze with Payal's, my voice tinged with confusion and frustration. She was no stranger to the questions brewing within me and she met my gaze with an understanding that could only come from shared history and trust.

"How much do you know?" she asked, her voice burdened with the weight of the revelations hidden away for so long. The question hung in the air, a plea for clarity amid a storm of uncertainty.

"Everything," I replied and the admission cracked the dam that had held back my emotions. Tears welled up in my eyes, spilling over onto my cheeks. It was a moment of vulnerability, one where the rawness of my feelings could not be contained any longer.

We sat amidst the echoing silence of the cafeteria, where conversations flowed around us, but our world had narrowed to that tiny table. Payal's eyes glistened with tears of her own, a reflection of the profound sorrow and remorse that had tethered her to a secret she could no longer keep.

She began to explain in a voice of regret, her words carrying the weight of days of silence. She admitted how sorry she was for not divulging the truth earlier, but she also offered a perspective that shed light on the complexity of her choice.

"It wasn't my place to share that information with anyone," she confessed, her gaze never wavering. "Kaya has confidently shared everything with me and I do not break promises. I also thought keeping it a secret from you was better for both of you."

During those moments, my perception of Payal underwent a profound transformation. She had always been my mentor, confidant and cherished friend, but now, she held a special place in my heart. Her actions were driven by a selfless and painful decision that aimed to protect Kaya, which was a testament to the depth of her character. The web of secrets that had tangled our lives was untangled, but the bond of friendship between us remained unbreakable.

After my conversation with Payal, I felt like a weight had been lifted off my shoulders and I had gained some clarity on the situation. However, I was now faced with a daunting task requiring me to take responsibility and make difficult decisions. I knew I needed a strategy, guidance and help to bridge the gap between Kaya and me. Turning to Payal, whose wisdom I valued, seemed like the natural thing to do.

I asked Payal for her opinion on the next steps I should take. As a woman herself, she could offer insights into the intricate complexities of Kaya's mind. I wanted to find a way to rebuild the bridge that had suffered so much strain. Payal's advice reaffirmed what she had said before, but it carried a newfound significance in light of our uncovered truths.

"Make an effort to spend time with her, take her out on dates, to the movies, on vacations—whatever you can do. Her soul and heart need healing and only you can provide that." Payal advised, her voice brimming with confidence.

Her words were not just suggestions but a chance for me to mend the broken bond between Kaya and me. They carried a weight of importance that I knew I couldn't ignore. It was a reminder that the path to rebuilding trust and love was paved with patience, understanding and the relentless pursuit of happiness.

I thanked Payal from the bottom of my heart, knowing that mere words could not express my appreciation. She had been there for Kaya when I had faltered, a steadfast pillar of support during the darkest times. Her counsel was a valuable asset, underscoring the importance of our friendship, which had evolved through shared experiences, challenges and profound moments of vulnerability.

Leaving the cafeteria, we returned to the busy office floor, our conversation serving as a beacon of hope amidst the uncertainties ahead. I felt a renewed sense of purpose, a commitment to do everything I could to bring joy and healing back into Kaya's life. Every step forward was a promise to mend the rift, nurture the love we once shared and rekindle the light of happiness that the shadows of the past had dimmed.

I knew that the journey to make Kaya mine forever was challenging. Yet, my determination and motivation were unwavering, driven by a love that had been tested and emerged stronger. I had a newfound sense of purpose and a commitment to stand by Kaya and be her unwavering support. My resolve was further fortified by the support of my family, who had been through the tumultuous events of our love story alongside me. Their blessings and encouragement were a source of strength and it was with a heart full of gratitude that I approached them for a heartfelt conversation.

The following morning, I gathered my family in our living room, where I stood before them, prepared to share the latest developments in my pursuit of Kaya. I implored them not to interrupt or object to what I would reveal. It was a moment of vulnerability, a turning point in our shared journey.

With honesty and transparency, I began to narrate the events that had transpired during my visit to Kaya's home. I was selective in the details I shared, for I understood the sensitivity of the matter and the need to respect Kaya's privacy.

"Kaya's father and I had a heartfelt discussion during my visit," I explained, choosing my words carefully. "He shared with me a part of Kaya's past, a burden she has carried for a long time, one that has weighed heavily on her heart."

I could see the curiosity and concern in the eyes of my family, but I continued, "Kaya is a strong and resilient girl. She has been working through her past and I am confident she will emerge stronger than ever. I promise that she will be okay, especially if she is with me."

The room was filled with a somber atmosphere as I shared what I had learned, providing a brief glimpse into the complexities of Kaya's past without delving into the painful details. My intention was not to burden my family with the specifics but to convey the essence of her struggle and her unwavering strength. Then came the pivotal moment when I unveiled Kaya's father's blessing.

"Kaya's father, who knows her better than anyone, blessed me to marry his daughter," I revealed, a warmth of gratitude sweeping over me. "He expressed his belief in me and his certainty that I would take good care of his beloved daughter. I have his unequivocal support."

The revelation of my discussion with Kaya's father added a layer of complexity to the narrative that my family found hard to grasp. Their concern was genuine and they sought understanding amid confusion. The bond between my family and me was strong, built on trust and unwavering support and they yearned for a path that would lead to my happiness and protection.

Understanding their need for clarity, I addressed their concerns. "I know this information is unexpected and confusing," I admitted, "but I need you to trust me and support my decisions. You're all concerned about my well-being and my future with Kaya. You want to ensure that she won't hurt my feelings again. I assure you that I will take care of everything."

My words were a testament to the sincerity of my intentions; my family listened, gradually finding solace in my assurances. Their love and concern for me were evident and the bond that connected us was unbreakable. My honesty and openness had bridged the gap of confusion and they now recognized that my commitment to Kaya was unwavering.

Their acceptance was a precious gift, allowing me to advance on my chosen path. My family was not merely my support system but the pillar of my strength. With their blessings and understanding, I knew that I was better equipped to navigate the complexities of my relationship with Kaya. As I concluded my conversation with my family, I felt a renewed sense of confidence to continue my pursuit of making Kaya mine, knowing that I was not alone on this journey.

In the days that followed my profound conversation with Kaya's father, my singular focus was on rekindling the spirit of the girl I once knew, the vibrant, energetic and effervescent Kaya who had lit up every room she entered. I longed to see her warm smile, which had the power to illuminate even the darkest corners and hear her laughter, which was infectious and could chase away any gloom. I missed Kaya, who was both shy and lively, always ready for an adventure. But I knew that for this transformation to happen, it needed to be on her terms, in her own time.

For the past few weeks, Kaya has been living alone at her family's village home. With newfound understanding and a promise to respect Kaya's haven in her village, I gave her the space she needed. I refrained from the constant texts and calls that had characterized my courtship, giving her the freedom to navigate her thoughts and emotions.

Meanwhile, I dedicated myself to making arrangements for the next phase of our journey. This involved ceaseless planning and discussions with both families and I kept Kaya's family informed every step of the way. Meeting Kaya's father and learning about his perspective and feelings helped me significantly. Kaya's family had promised to guard the secrets we now shared and had kept the nature of our discussions concealed from Kaya. She, in turn, had misconstrued my newfound restraint as a loss of interest in our relationship. She had started to think that I was finally ready to move on with my life.

As the days passed, I gradually grew closer to Kaya's family. They had embraced me as a member of their own and I made it my mission to bring moments of joy and laughter to their lives whenever I could. Kaya wasn't the sole sufferer in this tale; her family had journeyed through the same thorny path, bearing the burden of her suffering. My relentless pursuit of Kaya and my resolve to help her heal had earned their trust and affection.

With everything in place, from my extended leave of absence from the office to the destination of our imminent vacation, all seemed ready. After a week of negotiations with my manager and department head, I secured leave approval. Due to Kaya's disappearance and the ups and downs of my past two years, I had more than 50 days of paid leave I had accumulated.

Everything was set into motion, but one vital element was missing from the equation: Kaya herself. The question looming over me was how to bring her back to Ahmedabad and persuade her to embark on the adventure I had planned. The answer was not immediately apparent and I turned to both families for assistance and insight.

A pivotal weekend arrived and everyone came together as a united front, determined to reunite me and Kaya. The familial support was palpable, evoking a sense of nostalgia and surrealism. Observing them exchanging ideas and laughing at the silliest suggestions was a balm for their worries and pains.

My cousin, who had always been a source of creativity and spontaneity, posed a question that cut to the heart of the matter. "Is there something that Kaya cares about more than anything else in the world?" he inquired, his voice carrying a note of excitement.

My answer was unequivocal: "She cares about her family the most and I believe she still cares about me, even if she doesn't express it." The room buzzed with anticipation and it seemed we were one step closer to a solution.

As the collective brainstorming continued, my cousin leaped enthusiastically from his seat, exclaiming, "I have an idea that could bring her back to the city immediately if we wish." All eyes were on him, curious and eager to hear his plan.

"There are only two ways to bring her back," he continued, his excitement palpable. "Either I get admitted to the hospital, or I get married to another girl." His proposal was unexpected and I wasn't prepared for either scenario.

However, I quickly expressed my reservations. "It won't work," I countered, my concern for Kaya's well-being overshadowing any temptation to implement such a scheme. "She's smarter than you think and I don't want us to do something that could cause her more pain."

My cousin was determined and wouldn't give up. He insisted on explaining his idea in detail. "Listen to me," he urged. "If she still cares about you as you described earlier, I am confident my plan will bring her back to the city."

My response remained steadfast. "Bringing her to the city isn't the goal," I reminded him. "I need to convince her to go with me on a vacation. That's what truly matters." I gazed at my cousin, expecting him to understand my feelings and the situation's urgency. Deep in thought, he lowered himself into his chair, contemplating the right course of action.

The room had fallen into a contemplative hush after my cousin's proposal, with everyone weighing the potential consequences of such a daring plan. Kaya's father, a man who had transformed into a desperate father, his paternal instincts overriding his reservations, finally broke the silence. His voice was tinged with urgency as he offered a novel suggestion.

"It may work," he asserted his determination to ensure his daughter's happiness evident in his tone. "Somehow, if we can convince Kaya that meeting you one last time and giving the relationship one last chance might make her reconsider. But there's a condition, of course – if, after your one last effort, she still doesn't change her mind, you must promise never to contact her again and proceed with marrying someone else."

The gravity of the proposal hung heavily in the air. It was an extraordinary proposition that underscored the lengths a loving father would go for his child's well-being.

Accepting the gravity of the situation, I determinedly replied, "How and who would convince her of this?"

Kaya's elder sister was the first to offer a solution and her eyes held an unwavering determination. "I think I can help with that," she replied. She swiftly took her mother and left the room, clutching her phone to make the pivotal call to Kaya.

Though they departed on this critical mission, I was skeptical. My understanding of Kaya's decision-making process was extensive and her chances of yielding to such a plan were minuscule. The minutes ticked by, an excruciating wait filled with palpable tension. So unsettling was the silence that I asked my cousin to check on them not once but twice to alleviate the mounting anxiety.

After an interminable 15 minutes, Kaya's sister and mother returned, the gravity of the situation visible in the former's nod of denial. A sense of defeat washed over me and I couldn't contain my frustration.

"I told you it wasn't going to work," I exclaimed angrily and disappointedly. Despite my efforts, the plan seemed to be unraveling before my eyes, my confidence in Kaya's unwavering determination remaining unwavering.

My temper subsided and I looked at Kaya's father with determination. "There is only one way to make this happen," I declared, resolute in my decision. "I will go to your village and convince her to accompany me. If that's what it takes, I'll do it."

Kaya's father, skepticism etched across his face, questioned my resolve. "Do you think she'll agree if you do that?"

With confidence that bordered on stubbornness, I replied, "I will try my best, but if it comes to the worst, I'll use force."

"No," Kaya's father said with a loud voice. A shock wave rippled through the room at my bold statement and all conversation ceased. The audacity of such a suggestion left everyone momentarily speechless, grappling with the enormity of the decision.

The silence persisted, intensifying the tension in the room. After a few minutes, Kaya's father finally spoke, his voice laced with resignation. He requested his family's departure, signaling the end of this fateful meeting. The two families parted ways and as they left, it felt as though all my hopes, meticulous planning and earnest efforts had been dashed, leaving me with a profound sense of loss and desolation.

The passing days had brought with them a mask of normality as everyone in my life continued with their daily routines. The unspoken presence of Kaya loomed like a phantom, casting a shadow over my days. The situation was acknowledged and understood by those who cared about me. They recognized that only Kaya had the power to truly mend my heart and bring happiness back into my life.

Amid this surreal silence, I tried to maintain a veneer of normalcy. My friends and family could see my struggle and the gaping void in my life. They had wholeheartedly accepted that the key to my happiness was held by Kaya alone. As they fervently supported the idea of our reunion, they went to great lengths to achieve it, even resorting to cunning strategies and small deceptions to bring us back together.

One busy evening at the office, when my work entirely absorbed my focus, my mobile phone suddenly rang. The screen displayed a message notification. It was Kaya's father. I unlocked my phone and read the text he had sent. It contained a single piece of information that held the promise of change and a glimmer of hope amid the overwhelming despair - an address.

It was unmistakably the home address of their hometown, where Kaya had retreated to, seeking solace and refuge from her inner turmoil.

Later that night, I had a candid conversation with my father, who revealed that Kaya's father had relentlessly tried to persuade his daughter to reconsider. He had attempted every approach he could think of to reach her heart and mind. After numerous conversations and several attempts to convince her to return to our shared world, he had a growing sense of desperation. At that point, he believed it would take my direct intervention to reconnect with Kaya and touch her heart in a way no one else could.

The same night, I embarked on a journey, driving for six hours to reach Kaya's village by 8 AM. The long trip through the dark made me feel uneasy. I usually avoid traveling long distances at night, especially by car. The thought of driving on a poorly lit road, surrounded by darkness and only occasionally blinded by the headlights of an oncoming vehicle, scared me.

On this particular journey, I couldn't escape this unavoidable reality. It marked my inaugural solo long-distance nighttime drive and the anxiety that enveloped me was undeniable. My heart thudded in my chest as I took a moment to prepare myself. The passenger seat was vacant, a stark reminder of Kaya's absence, which had become the central theme of my thoughts during this odyssey. I couldn't help but reminisce about our shared moments, laughter and cherished intimacy.

The yearning for Kaya had become an obsession that left no room for other thoughts. I was prepared to go to great lengths to be with her, bring back the smile that had adorned her face and restore her happiness. My determination to win her back was unwavering, a resolute promise to myself that left no room for hesitation or uncertainty.

What haunted my thoughts was the stark contradiction in Kaya's behavior. At times, she seemed poised to take the next steps in our relationship, suggesting the possibility of a brighter future together. Her actions hinted at a profound affection, perhaps even love. The image of our happily-ever-after was a vision I held dear in my mind, a radiant beacon of hope that I clung to in those dark hours on the road.

However, the jarring reality was that Kaya had rejected my marriage proposal. The shockwaves of that rejection had rippled through my life, leaving my emotions in turmoil. She had communicated her decision without providing an explanation or offering any clarity. Instead, she had chosen to pass this heavy message on to her family, like a baton in a relay race, avoiding a confrontation. It was an act that had wounded me deeply.

Anger surged within me as I drove on that lonely highway and I could feel my thoughts and emotions spiraling out of control. My car abruptly stopped on the shoulder of the road and I found myself standing beside it, a lit cigarette between my trembling fingers. I gazed into the pitch-black night, my mind in turmoil, grappling with the overwhelming sense of rejection and frustration that engulfed me.

I fervently smoked my cigarette, exhaling the smoke in frustrated puffs. My mind was a whirlwind of conflicting emotions, struggling to understand Kaya's actions. I found myself lost in the dimly lit wilderness of my thoughts, contemplating every possible reason for her refusal. The profound mystery of her unspoken thoughts and feelings left me utterly helpless.

Was she afraid of being judged by her past? Or the wounds she carried from what had transpired were too deep to be exposed to the world. Whatever the reason, Kaya had chosen to remain silent, refusing to reveal the inner turmoil that held her captive. I was determined to uncover the truth, reach out to her and persuade her to open up.

My determination to remove the shadows from her heart intensified as I covered more distance. I was prepared to face the darkness that engulfed her, clear the confusion that concealed her true nature and close the gap between us. My unwavering commitment to solving the mystery of her mind overwhelmed me and I pushed through the lonely night.

Before 8:00 a.m., I reached her hometown, standing at her doorstep. The hometown was already busy bustling with people doing their morning chores and going to their farms. Most people in the town who saw me park my car at her home and walk to the door had their questions. Who was I? Why was I at her house? Was I a relative of hers? Was she expecting my visit? It was far scarier than approaching her father at her home in the city. Before I could knock on the door, she opened the door. It felt like she knew about my arrival; maybe she heard the voice of my car's engine or me locking my car, I had thought. She wasn't expecting me at her door; she was shocked and just stood there like a statue.

Togetherness

"Aren't you going to invite me in?" I asked calmly. I knew I had to be patient; she wasn't expecting me. She had not heard from me in weeks and I was unannounced at her doorstep. She did not answer.

"Kaya, can you please give me some water? It's been a few hours since I had any." I said with a fake smile. She just stood there looking in the distance, thinking about something. Thinking she was not listening to me, I tried to enter the door from beside her.

"Why are you here?" She asked, her eyes were already full with tears.

"I am here for you. No, I am here for us." I replied to her while wiping her tears. "Please let me in, I am tired. It was a long drive here! The people passing the house stared at us, trying to understand the situation.

"Please, Kaya. Everyone is looking at us; let's go inside and talk." I pleaded with a lower voice. She stepped back and let me inside the house, closing the door behind me. "Why are you staying here alone at this haunted house?" I asked while attempting a joke with the hope to cheer her up.

"It is not; it is our family home." She replied. My joke had made her laugh

Kaya stood in the middle of the home, her laughter echoing off the bare walls. She was laughing, but her tears were falling freely. Her shoulders shook with joy, but her face was warped in a mask of pain. She was laughing at the absurdity of it all. She laughed through the tears, defiantly declaring that she would not be broken. But the tears kept falling. They were tears for the life she had lost, for the dreams that would never come true. They were tears of the pain that she carried in her heart.

I did not stop her; I let her cry her heart out. I just stood there beside her until she slowed her sobbing. I looked for the water inside the house and after opening a couple of doors, I could find the kitchen. I fetched a glass of water for her. I sat her down, returned to the kitchen and drank a glass of water. I couldn't see any dishes or anything in the kitchen; it looked like she had not had breakfast.

"Please tell me, why are you here? Her voice trembled as she asked, "I told you we could not be together."

"I told you, I am here for us. And, let's be clear that you never told me yourself that we can't be together." I replied to her question, rejecting her denial. "I am not going anywhere until you come with me," I added while sitting beside her. Her crying continued.

"Please, stop crying," I asked with a heavy voice. I had a hard time controlling my emotions and making her stop. "Stop acting like a little girl," I added with anger. Nothing worked; I stepped outside near my car and opened the door. I sat inside the car, frustrated, thinking about how to console her; I lit a cigarette and started smoking while sitting inside the car.

After a minute or two, Kaya came out and said, "Please come inside the home and smoke; I know you don't smoke in your car," she said. Kaya had stopped crying and had washed her face.

I went inside the house without saying anything, finished my cigarette and washed my hands and face in the backyard. "Can you please pass me a towel?" I asked. She wasn't there in the yard; I looked for her and found her in the kitchen, preparing breakfast.

“What are you preparing? I asked her while entering the kitchen. It was a very small kitchen, making working together difficult for two people.

“Bhakri and Tea,” she replied. Bhakri is a staple breakfast in most Gujarati households.

“Make sure to control how much salt you add; I hate having anything salty first thing in the morning,” I tried another joke. She didn’t care to reply, but I was able to peek at a smile on her face. Though for a moment, a smile was there. I waited eagerly for her to finish preparing the breakfast; I never had Bhakhri made by her.

We finished breakfast and I hung in the courtyard, looking at the different trees and plants while she cleaned the kitchen. I was thinking of a conversation that would lead me to bring her with me on a vacation, but nothing concrete came to my mind. After hanging in the courtyard for a while, I went inside and sat there, scrolling through my Facebook feed.

“I love you, Kaya.” I ran to her and said, “Can’t we return to how we used to?

“I love you, too.” She replied, “I never stopped, but we can’t go back.”

“Why?” I added with curiosity, trying to understand the meaning behind her statement. “You just said you love me, but we cannot be together; why? I asked.

“It wouldn’t be right for you to be with someone like me.” She replied with a sincere voice.

I knew exactly what she meant by that. I knew where her mind and heart were, but I had made her father a promise never to let Kaya be aware of my knowledge of her dark past. If only I could tell her there was no point in keeping her past a secret from me.

"Whatever your reasons, maybe I will marry or wait for you forever. And this is my final decision." I replied, letting her know my conviction. She did not respond to that.

After sitting there for a while, I don't remember when I fell asleep. When I woke up, it was already an evening; she, too, had fallen asleep near the bed. She was sleeping like a baby, dreaming of a happy dream. I sat on the bed, looking at her peaceful face. Perhaps sleeping was the only time she wasn't forcing herself to act normal. Kaya's eyes were swollen and dark shadows hung beneath them, evidence of her frequent crying.

The passing of a tractor woke her up. "You could have woken me up," she said while rushing to stand up from the ground, but she lost her balance because of the numbness in her leg. Before I could get out of bed to help her, she fell backwards, landing on me.

I gasped as she fell, but she was so soft and warm that it was almost like being cushioned by a cloud. Her long hair cascaded over my chest and her lips brushed my cheek. For a moment, we lay there frozen, our eyes locked. I could feel her heart beating against my chest and smell the sweet scent of her hair.

"I am sorry," she said, trying to get up. But her hair was tangled onto my shirt's buttons. I slowly leaned in and kissed her forehead as she tried to untangle them. It was a soft, gentle kiss, full of promise, trying to remind her how much I loved her.

When she got up, I asked if she could make me tea. She agreed and went to the kitchen; I followed her. While she prepared the tea, I just stood there looking at her. Looking at her from the side, it felt like she had lost some weight.

"How much do you weigh right now?" I asked with curiosity.

"What kind of question is that?" she replied with a smile.

"I ask because I think you have put on some weight since we last met at my place," I replied with a smirk.

"No, I have not," she replied and continued preparing tea. When she wasn't paying attention, I held her by the waist and lifted her, "What on earth are you doing?" she shouted.

"I was just checking to see how much weight you had put on," I laughed.

"Put me down, this instance," she replied. I lowered her and she pushed me away and poured the tea into cups. We both drank the tea, looking at each other; whenever mine caught her eyes, she acted like she was looking at something else. I knew she was looking at me.

"Can we go for a walk?" I asked while putting my cup on the kitchen platform.

"This is not our city; everyone knows each other here," she replied. There was nothing else to do in that house and I wanted to explore her hometown.

"Can we at least go on a terrace? No one will see us if we are sitting on a terrace." I added my rebuttal to her objection. After thinking for a few seconds, she agreed. It was a beautiful evening; I could hear hundreds of birds flying while chirping and bells ringing far away in the temple.

"I like spending time here," she said with closed eyes, trying to feel the air breeze on her face. Kaya truly looked happy at that moment. Perhaps she was staying here to heal her heart and forget about her pain, I thought.

"Is that why you disappeared after our meeting?" I asked.

She took her time replying, "Not really."

"Then why?" I asked.

"I wanted you to find another girl, marry her and move on in your life.' she replied.

How could she not understand that was never going to happen? Did she think that I would have moved on that easily? I thought. I did not ask her anything after that. I just sat there enjoying the beautiful view of the town from the terrace and Kaya sitting in front of my eyes. I couldn't ask for more at that moment. We sat there for a few hours, watching the evening become beautiful.

It was almost midnight. "Are you hungry?" She asked. Her sudden reminder of food made me hungry. I nodded yes with modesty. She went down and I stayed on the terrace, thinking of how I would convince her to go on a vacation with me. I had no plan of action but hope. I hoped she would listen to me, knowing her well enough to prepare her for my planned adventure. The night is still young and I can do it, I said to myself before heading down.

We ate dinner, finished chores and sat in the courtyard. I smoked and Kaya sat beside me, reading something. Finishing my cigarette, I washed my hands and face and headed toward the room she had prepared for me. I wanted to talk with her about the vacation, but she focused on reading. I couldn't bring the vacation to her knowledge. After some time, she put her book aside and came to where I was sleeping.

"When are you going back?" She asked. It was a question that feared me the most.

After thinking for some time, I replied. "In a few weeks. I am on vacation and will stay with you for a few more days."

"Stop lying," she replied. "You say you are on vacation but have no change of clothes."

That never crossed my mind. I was planning to spend a few days with Kaya, but I had no change of clothes. In a rush, I had left without taking anything; it was an unplanned trip to her hometown. But how could I tell her that? I was embarrassed by her remarks.

"Well, that is a good question. I thought you would help me with that." I said, trying to hide my embarrassed face and covering for my stupidity. She smiled and headed to a room filled with all kinds of cupboards and drums; it felt like a storeroom of the house. She came back with an old T-shirt and track pants.

"These are my father's old clothes we keep here; see if they fit you." She handed me the clothes and went to her room. I changed into clothes, the night dress for me that night. After some time, she returned and started laughing. Her voice was so loud that every one of the neighbors would have heard her. Kaya couldn't stop laughing. Her laughing was contagious and after seeing her laugh nonstop, I joined her. I was truly happy; what my deliberately delivered jokes were not able to accomplish was achieved by my inability to fit into her father's old clothes.

She asked me to remove the T-shirt and that she would find something bigger. I tried removing the T-shirt, but it was so tight that it was impossible. I struggled for a while but was tired; I could not stretch my arms above my chest height. Looking at me struggling with removing the t-shirt, she offered help. Her laughing didn't stop at all.

I asked her to stand on a chair to pull the t-shirt from above my head. There were no chairs in the room, but there were a few empty drums; she bought one drum near me and stood on top of it. She pulled the t-shirt upwards and I forced my body and hands downwards. After struggling for a few seconds, I could free myself from the t-shirt, but the strength of getting that t-shirt out of my body imbalanced Kaya, who was standing on the unstable drum. She was about to fall, but I caught her in my hands before she could.

The funny situation turned serious; in that instance, the pace of our heartbeats increased and she could see and feel goosebumps on my uncovered shoulders and chest. As I carried her to her room, the sensation crossed my body. We had exchanged many intimate moments, but these feelings and sensations differed from those we experienced in the past. Controlling my emotions was taking everything I had in me; I put her in her bed and turned to go outside the room.

Before I could go out of her reach, she caught my hand and pulled me towards her. Her sensual touch on my chest and shoulders felt like an electric current passed through the veins inside my entire body. She sat on the bed and blessed me with kisses on my neck, chest and shoulders. She had forgotten all her pain and suffering at that moment, becoming the Kaya I knew from the past, Kaya, who was confident and adorable. It had been more than two and a half years since I had felt these emotions. Instead of controlling my feelings, I let them loose.

Kaya's eyes had become pools of desire, reflecting the longing that mirrored my own. Her fingers, trembling slightly, reached out to graze my cheek, tracing a path that ignited a spark of electricity between us. Her touch was a delicate whisper, a silent plea for more.

I couldn't resist any longer. I leaned and my lips met hers in a tender, passionate kiss. It was a slow, unhurried exploration of each other's mouths, a silent exchange of emotions that had remained unspoken for far too long. Her lips tasted like the sweetest nectar, a flavor that was uniquely Kaya.

As our kiss deepened, a soft moan escaped her lips and I felt her hands slip around my waist, pulling me closer. The world outside faded away, leaving only the two of us in this cocoon of desire and affection. Every brush of her lips against mine sent shivers down my spine and I pressed my body against hers, the heat between us undeniable.

Breaking the kiss, I traced a path of soft kisses along her jawline, down the curve of her neck. Kaya tilted her head to give me better access, her breath coming in shallow, erratic gasps. Each kiss was a testament to my love and longing, a promise of the passion that simmered beneath the surface.

My hands, trembling with desire, slid along the curves of her body, exploring every inch of her with reverence. The fabric of her dress felt like a barrier, an obstacle I couldn't bear. I unbuttoned it slowly with unpracticed hands, revealing the soft skin beneath. Her eyes never left mine, her gaze filled with trust and anticipation.

With the dress finally removed, Kaya stood before me in the soft glow of dim light, her beauty illuminated like a work of art. Her body was a canvas of desire, bathed in the silvery moonlight. I couldn't help but admire her, my hands trailing over her curves as if committing every inch of her to memory.

Kaya's hands found their way to my back and she began to pull me towards her, our bare chests pressed together, skin against skin. The heat of her body against mine sent a surge of desire through me and I kissed her with renewed passion. I took a moment to appreciate the sight before my lips descended, leaving a trail of kisses and nibbles that made her gasp and arch against me.

Time seemed to stand still as we explored each other's bodies; the outside world faded into insignificance. The soft caress of fingertips, the passionate kisses and the whispered declarations of love deepened our connection. The night was ours and the love I shared was a fire that burned bright. Our bodies moved in harmony, our hearts and souls entwined in a dance of longing and fulfilment.

As the night wore on and the moonlight burned low, Kaya and I found ourselves wrapped in each other's arms, sated and content. The room was filled with the soft, rhythmic sound of our breathing, a testament to our profound connection.

In the quiet moments that followed, her fingers traced lazy patterns on my skin and I nestled closer, my head resting against her chest. She gently kissed my forehead, whispering words of love and devotion into the night.

She whispered, “I love you,” music to my ears, filling my eyes with tears. Reminding me of our first kiss in the office pantry.

I embraced her tightly, replying, “I love you too, Kaya.”

Our meeting after months ended in a togetherness filled with passionate love.

As the night deepened, Kaya and I remained wrapped in each other's arms, the bed covers cocooning us in warmth. Our intimate connection had only deepened our bond and there was no place I'd rather be than there, with Kaya in my arms.

As we talked, my fingers traced soft patterns on her skin, eliciting gentle shivers running down her spine. Kaya's head rested on my chest, rising and falling with the rhythm of my breathing. The god of love had filled the room with the soft, soothing cadence of our heartbeats, a reminder of the love that pulsed through our veins. The world outside seemed distant and the only reality that mattered was the two of us, entwined in each other's embrace.

"Kaya," I whispered, gently brushing her ear with my voice.

She lifted her head, meeting my gaze with eyes shimmering in the moonlight.

"Our families, Kaya, they've accepted us without hesitation. They've supported us through thick and thin and I couldn't be more grateful."

Kaya's eyes reflected the same sentiment, a deep emotion shining. "It's true. I never imagined they would be so understanding, so loving."

I leaned in and kissed her forehead.

Her fingers tightened around me, a silent affirmation of her words. "My family has been my anchor. Through every storm, every uncertainty, they were there."

In the gentle quiet of the night, we both began to share stories about our families, reminiscing about the moments that had shaped our lives. It was a conversation filled with laughter, tears and a profound connection.

As the hours passed, I realized that we were no longer two separate individuals but a united force, ready to face the world together. And as we slept, intertwined in each other's embrace, we knew our journey had just begun. A journey that would continue to evolve, filled with new experiences, challenges and a love that would only grow stronger with time. Before I could fall into a deep, peaceful sleep, I texted my cousin and closed my eyes.

Kaya wasn't in the room when I woke up the next morning. I got up and started looking for her. I checked all the rooms, kitchen, backyard and courtyard, but she was nowhere to be found. Thinking where she might be, I looked for my phone and started calling her, thinking she might have run away.

She had run away from me a few times now. Her phone kept ringing, but she did not answer. I rushed to the terrace, hoping she might be there. I broke my toenail while climbing the stairs; she wasn't on the terrace either. My foot started hurting and bleeding, but I had to find her. I rushed back to the backyard and called her one more time.

I heard the sound of the main door closing; Kaya entered the home with a tray full of flowers and asopalav (Ashoka tree) leaves.

"Where is your phone?" I asked while controlling my breathing. Maybe she had run enough from me, I thought and with what happened last night between us, she may not think of running anymore. She knew I loved her and I had clarified that I wasn't going anywhere without her.

"I don't know; I was collecting some flowers in my neighbor's backyard." She replied and walked towards the kitchen. She kept the tray on the kitchen platform, entered the room we were sleeping in and came out while checking her mobile phone. "I did not wake you up because I knew you usually slept till noon." She added while walking towards me. "good morning to you, too." She said while kissing my forehead.

"Sorry, good morning," I replied, giving her a gentle hug.

"Kaya, can we go somewhere?" I asked her while eating breakfast.

"Where?" She replied.

I described to her the scenery of the vacation home I had booked for us without letting her in the whole vacation plan. "It is a very beautiful place just a few kilometers away from here and I want to see it while I can," I added excitedly.

She thought for a while and replied, "Ok, I will come, but we must tell my father." After finishing the breakfast, she called her father and got permission. I knew that he wasn't going to say no. Kaya had thought that we were going there for just a few hours and would be back before evening. My heart wanted to tell her the truth, but my mind made me keep it a secret. She took her purse, locked the main gate of the home and we headed towards the location in my car.

"Apart from my family members, you are the first girl who is sitting in my car," I said proudly.

"Only someone with a loose screw can think of going out with you." She replied like she didn't care. Her answer was instant like she knew what I would say. I kept driving. It was going to take about five hours to get to the location.

"How many girls have your family shown you for marriage? She asked with curiosity.

"I had stopped counting at fifteen," I replied. Kaya's eyes widened in shock as she learned that my family had recommended more than fifteen girls to me for marriage, but I had forced every one of them to reject me. She was eager to know why I didn't choose any of them. Her question was laced with jealousy and anger.

Her lips trembled as she spoke, her voice barely above a whisper. "Why didn't you marry any of those girls?" she asked. "They were all so beautiful and kind. Why did you force them to reject you?"

I could see the pain and confusion in her eyes. She was hurt and angry that I had chosen to remain unmarried, even though I had had the opportunity to marry one of many beautiful and desirable women.

I could feel the heat emanating from her body as she sat beside me. Despite her fascination with me, I sensed her anger and jealousy. I was at a loss for words. I needed to learn to explain to Kaya why I hadn't married any girls my family had recommended. I loved her and didn't want to hurt her, but I also couldn't bring myself to lie to her.

I took a deep breath and looked into her eyes. "I didn't marry any of those girls because I didn't love them," I said softly. "You are the only girl I have dated and loved."

With watery eyes, she took my arm. "I love you too," she whispered.

As we drove further away from the bustling town, the surroundings transformed, giving way to the serene countryside. The city and town's chaos and noise gradually faded into the background, replaced by the soothing sounds of nature. The sun began its descent in the sky, casting a warm, golden glow on everything it touched. It was a picturesque evening, perfect for the surprise getaway I had planned for Kaya.

As we approached our destination, Kaya couldn't contain her curiosity. She had been inquisitive the entire journey, asking questions and trying to guess where we were headed. A sly smile played on my lips as I watched her anticipation grow. We kept talking for nearly an hour before she fell asleep.

The sun shone through the window, casting a warm glow on Kaya's face. Her eyes are closed and her eyelashes flutter gently as the shadow of trees passes by and sunlight touches her eyes again. Her hair is spread like a halo around her head and her lips are slightly parted.

I can't help but keep staring at her. She looks so beautiful and peaceful in her sleep. I can't wait to show her the secret vacation I've planned for her. What I was varied of was her reaction; I could not think how she would react after learning the truth. I drove for hours, enjoying the scenery and her company.

Finally, we arrived at our destination, a small vacation home nestled amidst a lush landscape. "Where are we?" She asked while cleaning her eyes.

"This is it; this is the place I was talking about," I replied to her question with excitement.

The beautiful property was part of a cluster of vacation homes, each strategically spaced to offer families the utmost privacy. It was a haven for couples and honeymooners, a place where love blossomed amidst the beauty of nature.

The vacation homes were surrounded by tall trees that created a natural barrier, providing seclusion and intimacy. The gentle rustling of leaves in the breeze and birds chirping in the background set the stage for a romantic getaway.

As we exited the car, Kaya's eyes lit up with wonder. Her gaze swept across the meticulously landscaped garden, taking in the vibrant colors of the flowers and the neatly trimmed bushes. The sun's fading rays bathed the garden in a warm, ethereal light, casting long, romantic shadows.

We approached the vacation home and I couldn't help but notice how someone had taken the time to prepare it for our arrival. The front porch was adorned with a small, old table and a few chairs, inviting us to sit and savor the beauty around us. A small fireplace nearby hinted at cozy evenings, sharing stories and laughter.

Inside the vacation home, the air was infused with a fresh, clean scent, as if someone had opened all the windows earlier in the day. The interior was charming and welcoming, with tasteful decor that exuded warmth and comfort. This place was meant to create happy memories and I couldn't wait to start making them with Kaya.

Kaya's eyes sparkled with delight as she took in the surroundings. She turned to me radiantly, her face shining with happiness. "This is incredible," she whispered, her voice filled with awe.

I smiled back at her, feeling a surge of contentment. "I wanted to bring you here, to this beautiful place where we can escape from the world for a while," I said, my words laced with emotion.

Kaya's hand found mine and we walked further into the vacation home. The soft, muted colors of the interior created a calming atmosphere, making it feel like our private sanctuary.

As we explored the rooms, I couldn't help but feel a sense of excitement and anticipation. This was the perfect setting for us to reconnect on a deeper level, emotionally and physically. Our journey together had been a rollercoaster of emotions and now, it was time to rediscover the love that had brought us together in the first place.

Kaya's curiosity led her to open a nearby cupboard, where she discovered a selection of her clothes neatly arranged. Her brows furrowed in confusion as she glanced over at me. Without missing a beat, she opened another cupboard, revealing my clothes collection. Her puzzled expression deepened as she turned to me, a question on her lips.

"What is all of this?" Kaya asked, her eyes searching for an explanation.

I took a deep breath and approached her with a gentle smile. It was time to reveal the surprise I had been planning for weeks. "I'm sorry for not telling you earlier," I began, my voice filled with warmth and excitement. "But the truth is, we'll stay here in this vacation home for the next few weeks."

Kaya's eyes widened in surprise as she processed my words. Her initial confusion gave way to a mixture of emotions, including curiosity and anticipation. "Here? I can't," she said, her voice in denial.

I nodded, taking her hands in mine. "Yes, here," I affirmed, eyes locked onto hers. "I wanted to create a special getaway just for us, where we could escape from the world and focus on each other."

As Kaya absorbed the revelation, anxiety tugged at the corners of her eyes. She was beginning to grasp the depth of my intentions and seeing her react with such concern wounded my heart.

"But that's not all," I continued, my voice filled with enthusiasm. "I've also planned some adventurous activities for us to explore together. I want to make you happy, Kaya. Please forget about the past and fully embrace the present with me by your side. I want you to focus on us and nothing else."

My commitment to creating lasting memories with Kaya shone through with each word. I was determined to provide her with an experience reminding her of our love and bright future. Together, I wanted to rediscover the romance that had brought us together and this secluded vacation home was the perfect backdrop for our journey of reconnection.

Our vacation had just begun and the possibilities were endless. In this serene haven, surrounded by nature's beauty, Kaya and I were about to embark on a journey of rediscovering romance, passion and the profound love that bound us together.

"Who is in with you on this?" Concerned, she asked, "Please tell me the truth; I can cope with anything but a lie."

Sitting in the room, I finally told Kaya our elaborate plan to bring her here. I told her how our families came together on a mission to make us happy and how I asked my cousin to get our essentials, like clothes and food, for the vacation. Her expression shifted from surprise to contemplation as she processed the information. The room held a hushed silence as the weight of my words settled between us.

After deep thought, Kaya's eyes met mine and I could see understanding and appreciation in her gaze. She recognized that everything we had done was driven by a genuine desire for her happiness, a chance for her to find joy and peace. Her voice, when she finally spoke, held a touch of remorse.

"Sorry," Kaya whispered, her tone filled with sincerity. She acknowledged the concerns and worries she had caused to me, her family and everyone who cared about her.

Tears welled in my eyes as I reached out to hold her hand, grateful that she was finally willing to let go of the burdens weighing her down.

"No more apologies," I said softly, my voice filled with reassurance. "We're here to support and love you, Kaya."

A sense of peace settled over us as we sat together in that tranquil room. After sitting for some time enjoying each other's company, I headed toward the kitchen area to explore our food options. Fresh fruits, vegetables and milk were in the fridge and different instant mix packet options were in the cupboard beside the refrigerator.

"Kaya, are you hungry?" I asked from the kitchen.

She followed my voice to the kitchen, "Anything will work; I am really hungry, " she replied, pressing her stomach.

"I am not a good cook, but I can at least make a Maggie for us," I replied while showing her the packs of Maggie.

"Anything but that," she replied. "Lately, I have been eating a lot of Maggie and want a full lunch." She was really hungry and craving a nice full meal.

I could have done better at cooking. I wanted to cook her a nice meal, but I remember all the failed attempts at making anything from scratch and how all the food I prepared grossed anyone who had tried it.

"Well, you have two options," I said while giving her two choices. "Either we go out for lunch, or you prepare the food."

After thinking for a while, "How about you make the food, but I help you with cooking?" She offered a third choice. The idea wasn't bad at all. The nearest restaurant was almost 20 minutes from the vacation home, so I followed her suggestion.

"Let me see what we have here," she opened the fridge and took the inventory, deciding what could be cooked with the available ingredients. This wasn't in my planning at all. My instructions to my cousin were simple: get me some vegetables, fruits, juice and instant-mix food that I can cook by just boiling and some generic medicines. She took the cabbage, carrots and green chili from the fridge and looked at options available from the instant mix packets.

She picked something and asked me to wash the vegetables. I unbuttoned my sleeves, rolled them up and started marching at the order of her highness. I was enjoying my time with her. As I put the washed vegetables in a tray, she asked me to chop them.

"How?" I asked while looking at the cabbage and knife in my hand.

She took the knife from my hand and pulled the tray and cabbage to her side. Using her knife skills, she skillfully sliced the end of the cabbage and moved to cut the cabbage from the middle. She put the half-cut cabbage into the tray and started chopping the cabbage from one end.

"How you don't know how to chop a simple cabbage?" She asked while pointing the knife at me.

"Whoa, I went to study finance and statistics, not culinary art!" I replied while stepping back and taking control of the knife.

I started chopping the cabbage as I was instructed. As I finished the half she began with and was moving to the next one, she gave me the carrots, asking me to dice them. I knew how to slice or chop, but dice was a jargon to my limited knowledge.

"And how am I to dice the carrots?" I asked.

She then snatched the knife from my hands and started dicing the carrots, finishing the dicing in under a minute. I was learning the skills I never thought I would and as I spent chopping the green chili, she put something on the stove and covered it with a lid. The suggestion was that she would guide me with the dish and I would make it, but honestly, all I did was slice half a cabbage and two green chilies.

Intending to help, I took two dishes and spoons from the cabinet, put them on the dining table and sat there waiting for her to come with food; little did I know she followed me empty handed and sat beside me. She looked at me with stunned eyes; I stood up instantly, went to the kitchen and brought the pot and wooden spoon from the kitchen. I gave her the plate, served her whatever was in the pot and returned to my chair. The food was still hot; I blew air into the spoon and offered it to her. She took a bite and approved the taste with a beautiful smile and a thumbs-up sign. As I tested the dish, I realized what she had selected from the cabinet. She had prepared Upma with cabbage and a carrot. I cleaned the table and dishes as she sat outside in the garden.

It was a beautiful day; the cold breeze on a sunny day sometimes brought leaves and dandelion seeds with them, spreading the smell of the flowers in the whole surrounding. She looked in the distance, lost in her thoughts, when I came outside to where she was sitting.

"Kaya." I said, breaking her thoughts, "Let's go; we will be late if we don't leave now."

"Where are we going now? I thought we were staying here." She replied to my question.

"Please stand up and get changed into something comfortable. We are going for a hike." I replied while pulling her from the chair and pushing her forcefully to the room.

"Why can't we just stay here? It is so beautiful here." She kept complaining while changing.

"We are here on vacation, Kaya. Let's explore this temple I have heard of." I replied while checking the battery in my camera. We were headed to a remote hiking trail that leads to an ancient temple. The temple is known for its peaceful and beautiful surroundings that attract those seeking adventure and those needing solace. The stories about the temple emphasize its calming qualities and ability to soothe the soul. It is a perfect place for Kaya, who is in the middle of healing her mind and soul.

I couldn't resist admiring her beauty as she exited the room. She looked beautiful and fit in her tracksuit.

"I am falling for you all over again," I said with flirtatious intent. "You are looking beautiful."

"I know." She replied while blushing, turning her cheeks red.

As we embarked on the journey to the temple, I adjusted my sunglasses and felt the camera's weight around my neck. This hike was more than just walking; I wanted to capture every moment, especially when Kaya interacted with nature with her infectious enthusiasm. I noticed that sometimes she would get lost in thought, but today, it felt like she was present and cherishing every step, laugh and discovery she made.

As Kaya walked ahead, she was surrounded by nature's colors. The green trees were dotted with vibrant wildflowers and the chirping of birds and the distant sound of a bubbling stream filled the air. She stopped in wonder every few steps, sometimes leaning down to examine a peculiar-looking flower, its petals shimmering with afternoon dew. At other moments, she gazed into the distance, pointing towards the tiny structures below - the town, looking almost toy-like from this height.

I took these opportunities to capture her in candid shots. The joy in her eyes, the childlike curiosity, the moments where she seemed lost in nature – I wanted to freeze them all in time. There were moments, of course, where I was no longer the observer but the subject, as Kaya would playfully grab the camera and insist on taking my picture.

As we continued our ascent, we crossed paths with other couples. Some were young, mirroring our excitement, while others were older, their faces etched with lines of wisdom and years of shared memories. We'd exchange smiles, sometimes even sharing brief anecdotes or receiving tips about what lay ahead.

After a beautiful hour that felt endless and fleeting, we finally arrived at our destination. The temple stood before us, a timeless masterpiece, appearing as though it had risen from the very earth it was built on. Wild vines adorned the walls, weaving intricate patterns that seemed to tell tales of a bygone era. The temple's architecture was a mystery, with no inscriptions or hints about its creators or the deity it was built for. It was as though nature herself had created this sanctuary.

The scenery surrounding the temple was just as captivating. Vast gardens covered in many colorful wildflowers swayed gently in the breeze, creating a beautiful sight that stretched as far as the eye could see. The fragrant aroma was intoxicating, combining freshly mowed grass, blooming flowers and the unique scent that old stone structures ooze. Walking through the temple, we ran our fingers over the rough walls, feeling the carvings worn away by time. We were drawn to explore every corner, listening to the whispers of the walls that seemed to hold secrets.

We went to the temple's old stairs; Kaya held my hand, warming me while we sat on the cold stone. We didn't speak, but the silence said a lot. The peacefulness of the place surrounded us and time felt slower.

The sun lazily moved across the sky, painting everything golden. We were lost in our thoughts, our minds wandering yet anchored to the present by the beauty surrounding us. The outside world, with all its chaos and noise, felt like it was light-years away.

I paused for a moment to take a closer look at Kaya. Her face, illuminated by the soft light, appeared more radiant than ever. All the worries and stresses that often clouded her features had melted away and her face now bore a look of pure bliss. Looking at her cheery side and smile on her face made me genuinely happy.

As we descended toward the vacation home, the evening sky painted a canvas of deep oranges and purples, casting long, tranquil shadows over the path. The chirping of evening crickets began to fill the air, harmonizing with the distant hoots of owls. The world we knew gradually became focused, but the temple's magic, with its untouched beauty and the moments we shared, would forever remain etched in our hearts. As the sun set and darkness fell, we were reminded that while photographs may fade and memories may become hazy over time, the strong connection we felt with nature and each other will always guide us back to that forgotten temple. This connection is something we cherish and hold dear and it will never be lost.

We walked towards the vacation home, holding our hands. We saw an envelope and a small flower bouquet near the door as we reached the vacation home. We took the envelope and bouquet and entered the house. Kaya enjoyed the fragrance of the flower as I opened the envelope.

"It is an invitation to a party from someone celebrating their 50th marriage anniversary," I told Kaya while reading the letter.

"Should we go?" After thinking for a while, Kaya asked.

"I think we should," I replied to her question. "Whoever they may be, they are very generous." It was a handwritten note and the couple celebrating the anniversary who had invited us had also thought that the strangers might need a little encouragement; hence, they sent the flowers with the invitation.

We freshened up, put the camera and everything else inside the home and headed towards the location from the invitation. The celebration was taking place just a few vacation homes down the line. When we reached there, we saw many other couples like us invited similarly. The home's garden was filled with couples sitting in a circle with a small campfire. Most of the couples were in their late twenties or early thirties. There was no way some couple sitting there was celebrating their 50th marriage anniversary. The atmosphere of that vacation home was inviting, with people talking with each other and exchanging their relationship and marriage stories.

After sitting there and chatting with other men, I walked towards a corner for a quick smoke; I was glad I had company from other guys who also smoked. "Hey, gentlemen, cigarettes are not allowed in here." Someone shouted from afar.

We saw an older man coming out from the home, supporting his wife. Everyone smoking, including me, put out the cigarettes. We felt embarrassed. The older man sat her wife down where most were sitting in the circle and came to us.

"If you want to smoke, light a cigar. My wife hates cigarettes." He added and started laughing. Understanding the joke he just delivered, the entire garden filled with laughter. We joined others and the couple of honor in their celebration.

We learned that he owned most of these vacation homes and has been living in that home with his wife for the last ten years. After the celebration, we had dinner, sat there for a while and talked with the old couple, hearing the stories of their fifty-year-long marriage. We thanked the couple and took our leave.

It was almost midnight and the entire property seemed alive, illuminated by countless fireflies. Their soft glow – yellow, green and pale red – painted a picture straight out of a fairy tale. We paused, taking in the mesmerizing scene, as other couples, too, stopped to admire the natural spectacle.

Pulling Kaya close, I whispered, "I love you." It felt like the perfect moment.

She looked at me, her eyes reflecting the glow of the fireflies. "I love you too," she replied softly. "This... this right here is the most beautiful place I've ever been."

The night had worked its magic on us, binding us closer with its simple yet profound beauty. As we made our way back,

I realized that the most unexpected encounters can sometimes lead to the most unforgettable memories.

It had been over two days since we last heard from our families. My only conversation with one of my family members was when I asked my cousin to help us gather our clothes and other necessities. Kaya had to seek permission from her father before joining me from her hometown.

As we sat in the garden, we relaxed our tired legs and I asked Kaya if she wanted to join me on a call with my family. She smiled, "I would love to and I haven't talked with them." I called my mother's phone and we talked for almost thirty minutes, sharing what we had been up to in the past two days. Kaya participated in the conversation as if she was already a part of the family, answering everyone's questions. It was hard to believe that this was the same girl who had rejected my marriage proposal just a few months prior and had disappeared from my sight, locking herself in her hometown home. I asked if she wanted to talk to her family.

"No, I will call them tomorrow morning; they must be sleeping by now." She replied while walking inside, planning to go to bed.

I followed her inside and locked the door behind me. After a long day of adventuring and exploring, Kaya took a shower. She took her night dress and went for a shower as I sat on the bed thinking about tomorrow. I had planned another adventure for us, especially for her, which I thought she would love. I wanted to make every single day of our first vacation a memory that we could cherish for future decades, similar to the old couple celebrating their golden jubilee, telling the stories of their most cherished moments with light and love in their eyes.

Water running and droplets splattering against the tiled floor created a soothing background score for the quiet evening. A few minutes later, she emerged from the steam-filled bathroom, enveloped in the scent of her favorite jasmine. She wore a delicate white silk top paired with matching shorts, its fabric accentuating her natural grace. The attire subtly shimmered in the room's dim light, giving her an otherworldly appearance.

I couldn't help but pause and admire her. As my gaze traveled from her face, taking in the softness of her features, I noticed the water droplets on her ears and chin. They flowed down from her neck, navigated the gentle curve of her collarbone, meandered past her chest and finally disappeared as they reached her belly. It was as if each droplet told its own brief story of its journey across her body.

Her skin, still flushed from the warmth of the shower, contrasted beautifully with the white silk, making her glow like a moonlit night. Her hands, always so soft, seemed more tender and her legs, with their natural curve, took on an allure of their own. She seemed like an ethereal being, a mix of vulnerability and strength right there in front of me.

I saw a mischievous look in her eyes - a playful spark I had grown fond of. She came closer, her wet hair leaving water droplets behind her. Suddenly, she playfully tossed her hair and its damp strands brushed against my face, making me laugh gently.

She turned around and I saw she only wore a top and nothing beneath. There was a delicate chain around her neck with a small clasp, which she asked for help with by tilting her head. Without saying a word, she tilted her head to the side, allowing me better access and quietly asked, "Can you help me with this?"

Rising from the sofa, I played her game, faking a deep bow, "Of course, your highness! Your wish is my command."

My fingers brushed against her soft skin as I tried to undo the necklace's clasp. Her proximity made my heart race and her presence felt overwhelming, like being swept away by a gentle current. I finally freed the chain by taking a deep breath to calm my nerves, I whispered, "You look incredibly beautiful, Kaya, " as it slithered away from her neck.

Her face, already radiant, now held a soft blush. She turned, meeting my gaze with those deep eyes filled with gratitude, love and a hint of that ever-present mischief. The night was still young and the air was thick with unsaid words and emotions waiting to be explored.

"Thank you," she said, her voice barely above a whisper. It wasn't just a thank you for the compliment or helping with the chain, but a gratitude for the moment, the connection and everything unsaid between us.

I would be lying if I said I did not want her then, thinking she was tired and needed a good night's sleep; I controlled my emotions. Kaya's appearance, composure and overall aura completely captivated my mind. There was an undeniable magnetic attraction that I felt towards her. However, a part of me cautioned that she may be tired from all the day's activities. Despite my burning desires, I consciously decided to prioritize her sleep.

I shook my head slightly and reached for a towel, hoping that a cold shower might be the solution to distract my emotional mind. The sound of water cascading down the tiles provided temporary relief, but her image persisted, floating in the frame of my thoughts - stubborn and ever-present.

After what felt like an eternity, I finally emerged from the shower. I was dressed in nothing but a towel wrapped around my waist, exposing my torso. Walking back into the living room, I saw Kaya lost in a book. The gentle glow of the lamp illuminated her features, casting beautiful shadows that accentuated her curves. She looked almost ethereal, her petite frame magnified by my admiration.

I felt a sudden rush of emotions that threatened to overcome me. To avoid being swayed by her charm, I left the living area temporarily and went to the bedroom. Once there, I changed into my night attire and took deep breaths to calm myself. When I felt composed enough, I went back to the living area to ask Kaya about the book she was reading, now curious about it.

Leaning in, I asked softly, "What book are you reading?"

Her lips met mine, rendering words irrelevant. The book she had been reading lay forgotten, discarded to one side. She pulled me closer, merging her warmth with mine. Any resistance I had built melted away as our intensity reignited. The passion, zeal and longing were palpable. Each stolen glance and lingering touch fueled the fire between us.

After what felt like hours but was probably only minutes, I carried her in my arms effortlessly, with each step towards the bedroom punctuated by her soft sighs, her usually white cheeks turned red and buried in my neck. A thin glow of perspiration adorned her skin, making it glisten tantalizingly. Every aspect of her, every breath, every heartbeat drew me deeper, trapping me in a dance of love and desire. The first night of our vacation and togetherness was still young and we were willing and ready to get lost together.

Acceptance

As Kaya's eyes slowly opened, she was greeted by the sweet melodies of the morning birds. The delicate rays of sunshine seeped through the curtains, casting a warm golden hue across the room. I stirred beside her and she leaned over to plant gentle kisses on my cheeks.

"good morning," I whispered sleepily, snuggling into her lap.

She blushed and pulled the blanket over herself, covering her exposed body, looking shy. I kissed her slowly and passionately, enjoying the taste of her lips. When we finally stopped kissing, she whispered the three magical words that made my heart race.

"I love you," she confessed, her voice filled with the warmth and affection only she could bring.

We lay there for a while, wrapped in each other's embrace, enjoying the peaceful moment. After some time, she exited the bed and walked to the bathroom to start her morning routine. I took advantage of the moment and checked my social media feed, scrolling through my friends' latest posts and updates.

A few minutes later, she appeared again with a cup of tea she had prepared for me. I gratefully accepted it and went to the garden to enjoy tea and a cigarette while basking in the morning sun. The garden of the vacation home was a tranquil haven illuminated by radiant light. The manicured landscape was a testament to the devotion and care that the owners had put into it, creating a peaceful atmosphere that we were fortunate to savor.

Kaya gradually recovered her old self and her laughter and sense of humor illuminated our shared moments. However, there was still one question lingering in my mind - one that had the power to change our lives forever. I wondered if she would say yes if I asked her to marry me. Somewhere deep within me, I held a flicker of doubt, fearing that she might reject my proposal. That was why I was waiting for the perfect moment to ask when her heart was open and filled with happiness.

I returned inside and went for a shower. I was thinking of the day before us and what we could do today. There were many options; we could stay home and relax or explore the vacation home property and nearby surroundings. There were many beautiful spots to explore, mostly the temples and river banks. I got ready and sat on a sofa, asking Kaya to do my hair. As she did my hair, I enjoyed that moment with my eyes closed; at that moment, I was living yet another of my fantasies - Kaya doing my hair in the morning. These small things were very important to me, making my life happy and peaceful. Whenever she was around me, I felt at ease knowing she was safe and comfortable, at least in my eyes.

I suggested we explore the vacation home's surroundings. Despite spending two days at the property, we had yet to have a chance to explore its full potential. Judging by the stories we had heard from other couples and the glimpses we had seen the previous night, there was plenty to see and do.

We were staying at a vacation home with many great features, including a swimming pool, a small barn for horses and cattle, a beautiful lake a few kilometers away and plenty of activities nearby. I had a special surprise planned for Kaya, a horseback riding experience that she hadn't known about yet and I was very excited to share it with her. We began our day by visiting the horse barn as she had agreed. The experience and scenery were something we couldn't have found in the busy city. While we occasionally spotted a horse there, seeing them running loose in their safe place was something we had only ever seen in movies. A small trail to the barn that could only fit one car had beautiful jasmine trees on both sides, creating a beautiful arrangement of green and white.

We wanted a glimpse of the beautiful foals we had heard of during our exploration. We were thrilled to see two energetic little foals as we neared the barn. Watching them frolic in a lush, grassy and fenced hay-filled area was an absolute joy. Their playful and spirited energy was contagious and we couldn't help but smile, watching them play with each other.

As Kaya's eyes caught a glimpse of the baby horses, they sparkled with delight and she expressed her desire to get closer to them. Though hesitant, she felt excited and attempted to chase after them for a few minutes. However, she soon found herself out of breath and with a slightly sad expression, she returned to me.

The considerate barn caretaker noticed Kaya's longing and handed her a little pile of hay. He explained to her that offering hay or grass to the foals was the best way to gain their trust, as they were naturally wary of strangers. Kaya approached the young horses cautiously and held out the hay for them to nibble on.

Kaya's face lit up with joy as the young horses nibbled on the hay in her hand. She gently patted their foreheads and crests, forging a heartfelt connection with them. The moments she shared with them were pure innocence and happiness.

As we spent more time with the foals, a question popped into my mind.

"Kaya, do you still want to have children?" I gently inquired. Her face lit up with enthusiasm.

"Of course, I want to," she replied, her eyes excitedly shining. "I want an adorable daughter."

I couldn't resist teasing her a bit. "Just one?" I gagged, a playful grin on my face.

Her cheeks flushed with embarrassment as she responded. "Why are you asking me these questions? You already know my answers. We discussed this many times when we started dating."

I couldn't help but smile at her response. "I was just curious if you still wanted a daughter with me," I explained, feeling bashful.

With the topic of our future children settled, we continued to enjoy our time with the baby horses. The caretaker approached us, holding two sets of jackets, helmets and a saddle. He revealed that we were about to embark on a horseback riding adventure, which surprised Kaya.

As Kaya hesitated, I could see a mixture of apprehension and curiosity in her eyes. I encouraged her to wear the protective gear provided, even though she wasn't yet comfortable with horseback riding. I aimed to take photos of her sitting on a horse, so I wanted to ensure she was safe. After gentle persuasion, she finally agreed to wear the jacket and helmet.

With Kaya all geared up, I began photographing her with the foals. Some shots were candid, capturing her genuine interactions, while others were posed to create lasting memories. After a few minutes, the caretaker returned with two beautiful horses.

As we mounted our horses, the caretaker took the lead to guide us with the reins, ensuring our safety. Horseback riding was a thrilling adventure despite its challenges. We watched in awe as the foals ran around the horses freely and grazed on the lush grass, savoring the moment's beauty.

Time flew by quickly; before we knew it, it was well past noon. Feeling hungry, I asked Kaya if she'd like to head out for lunch. We walked hand in hand towards the parking area, talking about the baby horses and the charm of the vacation home.

After we reached our car, we drove to a nearby restaurant where I had arranged a surprise lunch date for Kaya. It was a small but thoughtful gesture to show my love and appreciation for her. When we arrived at the restaurant, I informed the manager about my reservation under my name.

The manager guided us to a table by the window, providing a picturesque view of the surroundings. We took our seats and a restaurant staff member approached us, delivering a stunning bouquet of roses to Kaya. Her face lit up with joy as she thanked the staff and me with a radiant smile.

"Thank you for the roses and for spoiling me," she expressed, her eyes filled with gratitude as she gazed at me.

The staff started serving an assortment of Kaya's favorite dishes without us having to place an order. Our table was soon full of delicious food beyond our capacity to finish. I had ordered every single dish I knew she liked. We indulged in a delightful lunch, savoring the flavors and enjoying each other's company. After we finished our meal, we returned to the car, with Kaya comfortably seated inside while I stepped out to have a cigarette.

"Why don't you quit smoking?" she asked, a hint of annoyance in her voice. "You know it can cause cancer and is not a healthy habit."

I took a drag from my cigarette and looked at her thoughtfully. "If you marry me now, I promise to quit smoking," I declared, my gaze fixed on her.

She sat in the car, her expression a mixture of surprise and contemplation. "What's next?" she inquired.

"I don't think we need to do anything too strenuous," I said reassuringly. "We can head back to the vacation home and relax.

There's a swimming pool we can enjoy, or we can explore the indoor gaming area. The choice is yours."

Kaya sat there, deep in thought, considering her options. The horseback riding adventure had been thrilling but also left us a bit tired. As she weighed her choices, she chose to go back to the vacation home, where we could relax in the living area, allowing our weary legs and backs to rest.

In the next few minutes, we returned to the vacation home. Kaya spent some time on the phone with her family, reassuring them of her well-being. They had been concerned about her despite my family's efforts to inform them of her whereabouts. During their conversation, she asked about each family member's health and the status of her father's store, displaying a genuine concern for their welfare.

As Kaya finished her call with her family, I couldn't help but ask her a question that had been on my mind for a while.

"If you care so much, why did you choose to live alone in your hometown in the first place?" I asked gently.

She hesitated for a moment, her gaze avoiding mine. Then, with a sigh, she finally spoke. "I don't want them to worry about me all the time; they have been through a lot these past few years because of me."

Kaya was struggling with overthinking; she didn't know what her family expected from her. They wished for her to be happy and cheerful, as she once was. They were always concerned about her, but Kaya also had some accountability for it. She could have stayed with them and tried to move on from her past, but instead, she chose the path of loneliness, forcing her family and loved ones to worry more.

“Can I ask for something?” Kaya asked, her voice serious.

“Sure, what do you want?” I replied to her, trying to put her at ease.

"Promise me that when I ask to stay alone at my family's hometown house, you will let me stay there without asking any questions," she replied, asking for a promise I wasn't ready to make.

"Why would I do that?" Trying to understand the meaning behind her request. "Why would you want to live alone? Why would anyone choose to live alone?" I added.

"There will come a time when this is the last thing I would ask from you," said Kaya confidently, like she knew the day would come. "You have to promise me."

Not understanding her request, I argued with her for a while. She told me her fear when I pushed for it. What she said was unimaginable for me at that moment.

"I promise you." I replied to her, "I hope for that day to never come."

As she lay in bed, she asked me to bring her the book she was reading the day before. I got up, gave her the book and headed to the garden with my camera. I sat under the shade of a tree, smoking and admiring the photos I had taken. The images were stunning; the trees, sky and colorful flowers looked even more beautiful through the camera's lens. I deleted duplicates or blurred photos and stopped at any that caught my eye. After scrolling through a few, I saw a picture of Kaya at the temple. She looked amazing in that photo: her bright, shining brown eyes and big smile, her hair floating in the air as she removed inches from her face. It was a candid photo and I had taken hundreds of pictures of her in just two days.

While scrolling through pictures, one caught my eye - a simple photo of a cactus; the next one, a close-up of its thorns. The clarity and focus of the pictures were exceptional, so I kept scrolling without deleting them. I came across photos of a night where thousands of fireflies were flying and sitting in the garden of our vacation home. I zoomed in on a photo of Kaya trying to catch the fireflies, a radiant smile on her face. She looked breathtaking. That picture reminded me of the Kaya I met that morning in the office pantry and the Kaya I went on a movie date with - pretty, innocent, shy, bubbly, cheerful, arousing and many others.

As I kept scrolling, I came across photos I didn't recognize. These pictures had subtle despair and pain about them. Perhaps Kaya had taken them as a way of coping with her pain, sadness and hopelessness. The views and thoughts that flowed into my mind forced me to light another cigarette. I sat there for a while, lost in thoughts, before entering the home.

I noticed Kaya fast asleep with a book as I entered the living area. It appeared that she had fallen asleep while reading. I gently closed the sliding door that separated the garden from the living room and placed the book on the coffee table. Afterwards, I proceeded to the bathroom to freshen up. Suddenly, I heard loud sobbing coming from Kaya's room. I quickly made my way to her and found her crying and muttering in her sleep. I tried to wake her up, but she continued to sob.

I woke Kaya up and she held onto me tightly while crying. It seemed that her father had been right when he told me about her struggles. These weren't just bad dreams but sudden episodes that took over her once happy spirit, leaving behind a different Kaya than I knew.

That afternoon, she sat silently on the couch, lost in thought and said nothing. I knew the path I had chosen for us wasn't easy, but seeing her like this was becoming unbearable. Doubts started creeping into my mind about my plan for our vacation. I even thought of getting medical help for her, but her father had already tried that. She was getting treatment for months and that didn't help.

That evening, I ordered her favorite food from the same restaurant where we had our lunch. I set up two chairs and a table in the garden, with one small candle. Trying to create a vibe of a candlelight dinner for her, I had hoped that my efforts would bring joy to her mind and soul. After setting up the dinner table in the garden, I called her out for dinner; she was still sleeping on the sofa. After waiting a minute or so, I went inside and woke her up, asking her to join me for dinner.

"I am not hungry," she said, ignoring eye contact. I sat beside her for a while, feeling lost, thinking all my efforts were going to vain. Though I hadn't lived her past life, I could still imagine her dilemma. She was fighting between her past and present, leaving no space for the future, a future I was working hard to create for both of us. I felt like crying, but I couldn't; I had to be strong for both of our sake.

After sitting there with her, I went outside and started moving food and everything else in the kitchen. I placed the table in its usual place and went to the garden for a smoke. She followed me outside, snatched the cigarette I had just lit and threw it away. She hugged me and started crying.

"This is who I am now." She said while crying, her tears dropping on my hands.

I couldn't say anything; I just stood there consoling her. After some time, she stopped sobbing and wiped her tears; she looked at me and wiped my face. She held my hand, walked to the kitchen, prepared a plate with food and offered me a bite. I smiled with watery eyes and took the bit from her hand; I did the same for her.

"Do you remember your message asking me to wait for you?" I asked Kaya as she prepared another bite.

"Yes, how could I forget." She replied with a small, gentle smile. "I waited for you to approach me for months, but you never did." Revealing the secret of her messages. "I knew you liked me and you usually stalked me. I shared my number with you, thinking that, one day, you would text or call me, but you never did. That was why I started sending you good morning and good night messages." She added.

I thought how stupid I was to assume that only I liked her and she never paid attention to me; I started laughing.

"You were a coward back then," she said, annoyed by my laughter.

"That I was back then," I accepted her allegations. "I often heard the stories of boys from our department or other departments approaching you and you always rejected them without giving them any opportunity or explanation. I was scared that if I approached you and you would have done the same with me, I would be the laughing stock amongst my peers and the team."

"I rejected them all because I liked you, you stupid," she replied. "I was head over heels for you from the moment I saw you for a week in the morning shift. I often tried finding your phone number but failed and Anjali helped me get your number."

"I waited for months for one response from you." She added with excitement in her eyes. "And, when that morning you replied, I almost shouted in my bed. I had just woken up and sent you the message, but when you replied, I thought this was the best opportunity to share my feelings."

Kaya continued with her story from our first meeting in the office, "When I saw you on the floor and asked you to wait for some time. I was calming and preparing myself in the girls' washroom. Initially, I only wanted to confess my feelings for you. I wanted you to know that I liked you, but I don't know what came over me and I couldn't stop myself from kissing you." Her cheeks turned bright red as she told the story.

"I am thankful that you kissed me that day," I replied to her, "that kiss changed my life forever." I pulled her closer and hugged her.

Before she could return to reminiscing about her life, I continued, "But why me?" I wanted to know the answer to that question. In the past, whenever I had asked this question, she always changed the subject or said that she would tell me some other time.

"I had my reasons," she said.

She tried avoiding the question, but I wasn't letting her do that this time; I wanted to know why she chose me. "You must tell me the real reason. Why did you like me over many other boys that approached you?" I asked.

After staying silent and putting her thoughts together, she said, "Because you liked me."

Before she could finish her sentence, I stopped her and asked her to tell the truth, "I am not buying that reason; you must tell me the real truth." My voice had a request in it.

"I am telling you the truth; stop interrupting me and let me speak." She replied with a grain of anger. "Because you liked me for who I was and not just my face and body. Every boy who approached me wanted to show their friends they were dating a nice girl. But you were different; you kept staring at me from afar, never approached me and whenever our eyes met, you always looked the other way, feeling like you were caught."

We finished our dinner and I started washing the plate and bowl we used. She sat on the kitchen platform as she continued with her story.

"What made me decide was when I learned that your friends and peers respected you." She added, revealing the most important part of her story. Her voice was calm yet confident.

"And how did you come to that conclusion," I asked.

"Most team leaders were fighting for the morning or noon shift, but I never heard your name in that list and all the boys that got transferred from evening to morning respected you. The most delinquent bunch from the evening shift had respected you the most." She added.

"Thank you for telling me the truth, Kaya," I replied; that was the only thing I could say.

We moved to the living room to continue our conversation and Kaya stepped into the bedroom to get changed. She returned a few minutes later, wearing her nightdress and saw the garden again filled with illuminating fireflies. Excited about the sight, she rushed to the garden with the camera and started clicking pictures. However, she could have been a more skilled photographer and most of the pictures she had taken in the past few days needed to be more focused and up to her standards. As she peered through the camera lens with one eye, all she could see was blackness, as the shutter was still closed. I removed the shutter from the lens and allowed her to play the photographer.

After a few minutes, she handed me the camera and started posing like a model. She asked me to take her pictures and I couldn't say no. She played the role of a bubbly Kaya and I continued clicking her photographs, directing her to change her poses after every few shots, acting like a professional photographer. She nearly lost her balance and almost fell as she attempted a difficult yoga pose, causing us to erupt into laughter.

After we moved inside, she went to bed. I sat beside her, holding her hands and gently patting her forehead until she fell asleep. When she was sound asleep, I stood up and closed the door quietly behind me. I had heard that a good night's sleep can heal any pain, but with Kaya, it was sleep that was bringing her pain. I wanted to update our families about what had happened during the evening, especially her father. He had requested me to inform him of any episodes she might have during the vacation. Kaya's father had entrusted me with his daughter, but although he knew I loved her and wanted to marry her, I hadn't proposed to Kaya and she had not yet accepted my proposal. After my conversation with the families, I changed into a nightdress and sat in the garden smoking.

The following days and weeks passed quickly as we explored the famous attractions and tourist spots nearby. Kaya was mostly her usual self, except for a few nights when she had painful nightmares that caused her to cry out in her sleep. It was heartbreaking to hear her cries, especially knowing the unfortunate truth behind those nightmares. I had kept Kaya in the dark about my knowledge of her past, which was much greater than she realized.

There were just a few days left in our vacation and I still hadn't found that opportunity to propose to her. That morning, while getting dressed, I picked up the red velvet box and looked at the ring, trying to make up my mind to propose to her. Kaya was acting normal and I thought today would be when I would propose to her. I quickly hid the ring in my pocket as she entered the room.

"Where are we going today? Kaya asked with curiosity while getting ready for the day.

"Parasailing," I replied with enthusiasm in my voice. However, Kaya seemed to have confused parasailing with paragliding and I had to explain the difference between the two activities to her. Even after learning the difference, she still seemed hesitant about being pulled by a boat on the water while flying in the air.

Kaya and I embarked on our final adventure together; I couldn't help but think about how I would propose to her. Scenes from romantic movies flooded my mind, but none seemed fitting, given the highs and lows we had experienced in our relationship.

Suddenly, my thoughts were interrupted by a call from Vijay. I answered the phone.

"I have Kaya sitting beside me and we're on speaker," I said, anticipating Vijay's tendency to use foul language. Kaya giggled, covering her mouth to stifle her laughter as she listened to me warn Vijay before he could speak.

"Hi, Kaya Bhabhi," he said, teasing me and laughing on the phone. Kaya joined in with a silent giggle that soon turned into laughter. Although Vijay and Kaya had never met outside the office, their conversations on the phone made me feel like I was listening to family members chatting. They mostly talked about me and my behavior during vacation, with Kaya often joining Vijay in his teasing. We spoke briefly before Vijay mentioned that he had something important to tell us.

"I am getting engaged next weekend and you both need to come." he broke the news like any other.

"Congratulations..." I was tempted to use profanity after being away from my colleagues for weeks, where such language was common.

Kaya followed me and congratulated Vijay, "Congratulations, Vijay bhai." After a few minutes of conversation, Vijay asked me to call him when I could before hanging up. I continued driving and looked at Kaya, asking for her hand in mine.

While holding hands, I asked Kaya "when we would have news to share like Vijay. Everyone around us is getting engaged, married and having babies."

The atmosphere around us suddenly changed from cheerful to tense when Kaya responded to my question with her own, "You already know about my situation, so why would you want to spend the rest of your life with me?" she asked seriously.

"Because I love you and want to spend the rest of my life with you," I replied, looking into her eyes. "I will never stop loving you and marrying another girl is out of the question. My family is aware of this fact and you should be too," I explained, making myself clear.

"You would never be fully happy with me. Someday, you will see me for who I am and other days, you might not be able to recognize me," she replied.

As I failed to comprehend her reasons, I pulled over to the side of the road. I retrieved the box from my pocket and handed it to her. "If you truly believe we should not get married, here is the ring I purchased to propose to you. Throw it out of the car and I will never ask you to marry me again." After a long silence, I composed myself and resumed driving.

She opened the box, took out the ring and kept looking at it.

I continued driving and expressing my feelings, hoping to reach her heart. "I love you, Kaya. I don't know how else to convince you that we are just perfect together."

She continued to stare at the ring; after a couple of minutes, she looked at me and started crying, "I only want one daughter." She said,

It took me a few seconds to understand what she meant. I abruptly stopped the car on the side of the road and asked her to confirm what she meant. "Do you mean you will marry me? My heart was pounding as she nodded her head in agreement and cried.

Over the moon with happiness, I jumped out of my seat and hit my head on the car hood. Unable to contain my joy, I leaned towards her seat and kissed her. "I love you, Kaya, thank you," I said while kissing her. I opened the car window and shouted, "I love you, Kaya." I had tears in my eyes, but they were tears of joy.

The entire way to our destination, I repeatedly sang the same words to her, like a song playing in the loop. As we reached the destination, I jumped out of the car and ran to her side of the door. I pulled her out of the car and wrapped my arms around her. She melted into my embrace, her arms tightening around me. I could feel her body's warmth against mine and her hair's softness against my cheek. I took a deep breath, savoring the moment. Our hearts beat in unison as we stood there, holding each other close. I felt completely at peace in her arms and knew we were meant to be together.

After taking that moment in, I bent down on one knee and asked her to extend her hand. As she extended her hand, "Kaya, I love you. You are the most amazing girl I have ever met and I can't imagine my life without you. Will you marry me?" I officially asked, my voice excited.

She nods her head and tears stream down her cheeks. "Yes!" she said. "Of course, I will!" She gave me the box and I slipped the ring on her finger.

We kissed! It was an electrifying moment when our lips met. Our shared connection transcended everything else and the world seemed to fade into the background. The passionate kiss left only the two of us entwined in the moment. As we parted our lips, the world suddenly roared back to life and we were welcomed with loud cheers from the other couples and families at the parasailing location.

We were overwhelmed with joy and excitement as we approached the designated spot for parasailing. Congratulations and well wishes poured in from those around us, adding to our bubbling anticipation for the adventure that awaited us. Hand in hand, we walked towards the launch point, ready to experience the thrill of parasailing.

Upon arrival at the check-in area, we were outfitted with harnesses and given a brief orientation on what to anticipate during our parasailing adventure. The sun shone brightly, casting a radiant golden glow over the immaculate lake ahead of us. Our hearts were pounding in unison as we boarded the boat, joining our fellow parasailers and the experienced captain.

Kaya stepped onto the platform at the back of the boat and gripped the bar with excitement and nervousness. I could feel her apprehension and it made me feel empathetic. However, the captain, a skilled professional in this exhilarating sport, gave the signal to start ascending.

We were lifted into the air as the winch started to pull the ropes. The initial feeling of being airborne was both thrilling and a bit unnerving. Kaya held the bar tightly, her knuckles turning white as she adjusted to the breathtaking view below us.

At first, she was visibly scared, but as the wind caressed her cheeks and the stunning scenery revealed itself beneath her, her unease gradually gave way to amazement and admiration. She began to unwind, her hold on the bar loosening as she began to appreciate the adventure.

As we soared higher and higher, we both burst into laughter, feeling the adrenaline pumping through our veins. We gazed at the mesmerizing view of the lake below, surrounded by lush greenery, with distant towns on the horizon. With each passing moment, our spirits lifted and we experienced an indescribable sense of freedom and vitality.

During our thrilling adventure, my overflowing emotions couldn't be contained. I repeatedly shouted, "I love you, Kaya!" Though the wind carried away my words, they echoed in our hearts.

After experiencing several awe-inspiring minutes, the captain finally initiated the descent. Slowly and gently, we glided back towards the boat, our hearts still racing from the unforgettable experience. Finally, we touched down safely on the platform, our feet again firmly on solid ground. We disembarked from the parasail, our faces beaming with the sheer exhilaration of the adventure.

Before leaving, we retrieved our camera from the boat's staff members; we were determined to capture the memory of this incredible adventure. With the parasailing chapter of our day complete, we made way for others eagerly waiting for their turn.

As we walked along the shore of the lake, we came across several small stalls selling various snacks. I asked Kaya if she felt like having some sweet corn. She responded with a smile and nodded, so we headed over to one of the stalls.

We sat by a peaceful lake, enjoying delicious sweet corn while chatting casually. We watched as other brave souls attempted parasailing for the first time, their happiness and laughter reflecting our sense of excitement. The day turned out to be a collection of unforgettable moments, each bringing us closer together and strengthening our bond.

“Remember when we went out on a movie date?” She reminded me of yet another cherished memory of ours.

“How could I forget that day? We almost kissed in public; our lips were just about to meet and I had to stop myself from kissing you.” I replied, feeling embarrassed. “I wasn’t brave enough to show my affection for you back then, but now it is a different story.” I leaned in and tried to kiss her again as she avoided another kiss in public.

"Why do your cheeks always turn red when I kiss you?" I asked her, my voice filled with curiosity.

She blushed even deeper, her eyes sparkling with mischief. "How am I supposed to know? I can't control my blood flow or see my cheeks when we kiss."

Sitting by the scenic lake, we savored the sweet corn, laughter and conversation. The sun's gentle descent painted the sky with hues of orange and pink, creating a soft, romantic glow that enveloped our surroundings. It was a moment straight out of a storybook, where time seemed to stand still and everything was infused with a dreamlike quality.

As we sat together, our hands entwined, my mind couldn't help but reflect on our beautiful journey, both literally and figuratively. Sometimes the peaceful and sometimes wavy waters of the lake perfectly mirrored our journey. It was one of those rare moments when words were unnecessary and we could communicate through shared smiles and meaningful glances.

We spent a long time enjoying ourselves and finally returned to the car and headed toward the vacation home. I started the car and the soothing sound of the engine became a backdrop to our contemplative silence.

I shifted my focus towards Kaya, considering whether we should disclose the thrilling news about my proposal and her acceptance to our families. It was a momentous occasion and we wished to celebrate it with our loved ones. Kaya reflected on the idea for some time, her eyes expressing warmth and contemplation.

She suggested, "Shouldn't we tell them this news in person?' Her voice carried a sense of respect for her family. Her idea resonated with me deeply. "Certain news is meant to be shared face to face, allowing us to witness the genuine reactions of those we hold dear." She added.

We had decided and now it was time to return to our vacation home. The sun gradually set, causing long shadows to stretch across the landscape and creating a serene golden light. The warm afternoon air had shifted into a cool, refreshing breeze as a reminder that evening was fast approaching.

Upon parking the car and opening the door, Kaya injected a playful moment into the situation as she made a charming request. She asked me to carry her into the house and I couldn't resist her lively spirit, so I willingly agreed.

With utmost tenderness, I lifted her and held her in my arms. Her laughter echoed around us as I carried her across the slider. Gently, I set her down on the sofa and her eyes shone with a playful gleam.

As I stretched out beside her and rested my head on her lap, I began to play with her silky hair. It was an intimate moment when time slowed down and the outside world faded away. In the warmth of her gaze, I searched for something words could not express - a profound connection, a shared journey and an unspoken promise of a beautiful future.

"What are you looking at?" Kaya asked, her curiosity shining through the tender moment we shared.

With a loving smile, I replied, "I am admiring your beauty." With a touch of cheesy charm, it was a simple and heartfelt compliment.

Our laughter filled the room, echoing through the walls of the vacation home.

There were just a few days left in our vacation; the time had flown by faster than we anticipated. There was so much more I wanted to explore with Kaya, but now I wasn't bound by time; she was mine forever and I had a lifetime to do that.

"Can I ask you something?" She asked, breaking my chain of thoughts.

"Sure," I said while looking at her.

"How much do you love your family?" She asked with seriousness in her question.

"What kind of question is that? I replied, "I love my family very much; everyone loves their family. What is the point of this question? Where are you going with this?" I did not understand why she asked me that question.

"What would you do if there comes a situation in the future when your family learns the truth about me? What would you do then?" She asked, looking deep into my eyes.

With her follow-up question, I understood exactly where she was going with her initial question. "That day will never come; my family loves me and respects my decisions." I replied while comforting her, "They love you and care about you and I am sure if they learn about it, perhaps they will shower you with love more than ever," I added.

She sat deep in her thoughts while I wrapped my arms around her and tried to reassure her. After thinking some more, she added, "What if they heard me crying in the middle of the night? What would we do then?"

"They already know about your nightmares, Kaya and they also know that you went through the treatment for the same," I replied to her question; before I could finish, she cut me off asking.

"How much do they know?" She asked with a worried face and with water in her eyes.

"Relax, Kaya. They don't know anything." I replied, telling her why and how behind her question. I let her in the story of me meeting with her father at his store when she had stranded herself at their hometown home. He wanted to tell my uncle and family the truth, but I had asked him not to. It wasn't our story to share; it was up to Kaya to decide if she felt comfortable with my family knowing about her past. My family's opinion of Kaya would not have changed after learning about her painful past, but I wanted Kaya to make that decision herself.

“My family knows that you started having nightmares after your sister’s death. Your father and I made up a story and for them, that is the secret of your past.”

Kaya looked at me and started crying.

“Anyone who doesn’t know, I plan to keep it that way only. It is better that way and when you are comfortable sharing with them, we will tell them together.” I added while wiping her tears.

I held her until she felt better. "Thank you, I love you," she whispered.

I kissed her forehead in response to her whisper. In that instance, someone knocked on the door. I stood up and opened the door, it was a delivery man with a package. It was a gift I had ordered for Kaya.

As I closed the door and headed back to her, “What is it?” She asked.

“A small gift for you,” I replied. She opened the package and looked at me.

“What is this?” She asked with a top and a short in her hands, her eyes shocked.

I had ordered her a black two-piece tanking. “Get dressed and let’s go to the swimming pool,” I asked her with excitement and playful eyes.

“I am not wearing this in public.” She said while putting them back in the paper bag.

“Yes, you are.” Pushing her to the bedroom, I said, "Get changed. We're leaving in five minutes. We only have an hour before the pool closes."

To get to the swimming pool at the vacation home, we had to cross a few other vacation homes as it was located at the end of the property. The pool was of medium size with shallow and deep lots, catering to experienced swimmers and those who want to enjoy the water. Overall, it was a perfect spot for couples who stayed at vacation homes looking for a fun pool experience.

I changed into my swimming shorts while she was changing in the room. In a few minutes, she opened the door and came outside, wearing a big white scarf covering her body from head to toe. She looked like a beautiful ghost in white and I couldn't help but laugh.

"I am not coming with you," She said angrily.

I apologized to her while trying to control myself, "I am sorry, Kaya, but you look funny in that scarf."

She joined me in laughing and we headed to the pool area. The warm glow of the sunset made the evening feel cozy and inviting. As we approached the pool area, we noticed that the pool, usually full of couples, was empty; no one was swimming. Perhaps the cold wind of the evening and cold water in the pool had scared me the most from using the pool in the evening.

"We are in luck," I said to Kaya. "We have the whole pool to ourselves."

I jumped into the pool and took a dip. The water in the pool was cold but not freezing. I invited her to join me and after looking around to make sure no one else was there, she entered the pool, removing her scarf.

Kaya's presence transformed the atmosphere as she walked in, wearing a tasteful black tankini that highlighted her graceful allure. The swimsuit was modest yet tantalizing, accentuating her radiant glow and showcasing the striking contrast of her luminous white skin against the dark fabric; usually, loose hair was pulled back into a bun, adding an extra layer of allure.

Her legs were soft and curvy, displaying her grace. She walked elegantly, drawing attention to her hips, which were hugged perfectly by her tankini, accentuating her natural curves.

Her smile was radiant and captivating, making her approachable and charming.

Kaya embodied beauty and confidence in that moment, leaving an unforgettable impression on anyone lucky enough to witness her charm. She left me completely captivated and deeply in love once again.

As Kaya approached me in the pool, her shyness quickly scattered and she became playful. We started in the shallow end, where she could comfortably touch the floor.

We laughed and played in the water as the sun slowly set on the horizon. Our playful splashing and teasing gradually became more serious as we gazed at each other beneath the surface. We had been yearning for this moment for a long time. We tried kissing underwater, but that wasn't possible for us; feeling the electricity of our love instead of worrying that someone would see us kissing in the pool, we let ourselves loose.

Our kiss continued, amplified by the water. We shared several more, each more passionate and longing than the last, our desire for each other real. The moments were unique and thrilling, with our lips touching in water. Our love spoke volumes in that kiss.

Each time Kaya touched my bare torso, she gave me goosebumps. We held each other in the quiet pool while the water sparkled in the fading sunlight. Time seemed to stand still as we enjoyed the closeness in those moments.

The evening sun finally set below the horizon, signaling the end of our time at the pool. We wrapped ourselves in towels and I noticed that Kaya was shivering. I offered my towel to her and we hurried towards our vacation home, nearly running.

As Kaya took a hot shower, I wrapped a towel around my torso and went to the garden for a smoke. Sitting alone in the garden, I lit a cigarette and enjoyed the cool breeze surrounding me. The night was quiet, except for the gentle rustling of leaves, which provided the perfect background to my deep thoughts. The cigarette burned steadily in my hand, its smoke rising and mixing with the night air. I took a deep breath in, feeling the smoke fill my lungs and then exhaled slowly, watching as it vanished into the night.

The garden around me was alive with fireflies, their blinking lights creating a magical dance. I was mesmerized by their beauty as each little light told its own story, flickering in and out of existence. A sense of calm washed over me as I sat smoking and watching the fireflies. All my worries about the past and future faded away, leaving me with a feeling of peace. As I took another drag of my cigarette, I knew I would carry this calm long after the fireflies had gone to sleep.

After finishing my cigarette, I went inside and saw that Kaya had finished bathing; she was breathtaking. She winked at me with a mischievous glint in her eyes and said, “I bet you can’t guess what I’m thinking right now."

"I know what you're thinking, my love," I whispered, my breath hot on her neck. "You're thinking about how lucky you are to have me in your life."

"That I truly am," she said, her voice soft and sweet. "There was also something else.”

I thought for a moment and realized what she meant. “Yes, I am ready!” I shouted with excitement and kissed her on the neck.

“You are going to make dinner tonight,” and she pushed me gently toward the kitchen. “And I'll take my Maggie with cheese." At that moment, Kaya was back to her true self. Cheerful and confident Kaya I once knew was standing in front of me.

I took a shower, got ready quickly and went to the kitchen to make Maggie . While I was preparing food in the kitchen, she came up behind me and started teasing me. Sometimes, she would pinch or pull my ears or kiss my back. She knew that I was enjoying her attempts at provocation.

In about ten minutes, I finished cooking and we sat at the dining table, talking and enjoying our food. "You are more lively than usual today. What is the occasion?" I asked Kaya.

"I am happy because we got engaged today!" She replied. "I think I, too, can have the life I once dreamed of. Thank you for that."

"No, thank you, Kaya. Your acceptance has filled my heart with boundless love." I said and we both leaned in for a cheesy kiss.

After finishing dinner, cleaning up and putting everything away, Kaya and I sat on the sofa chatting. I invited her to join me for my evening routine in the garden and she got up; I thought she was coming with me, but she went to the table where she kept her things and took the book before heading toward the bedroom.

"I want to finish this romantic chapter," she said, holding up the book. "Please come back soon."

I nodded and hummed while walking to the garden. I sat there smoking and checking my social media; as I scrolled through the updates of my family and friends, I thought that in those past three weeks, we had disappeared from the society we were living in. There was no real connection between our friends, colleagues and us; at least we stayed in contact with our families. In my quest to make Kaya herself, I was evolving around her life, preparing myself for the unknown future. I spent the vacation getting to know her emotional needs and learning how to support her while navigating her emotional ups and downs.

I finished smoking and headed inside. I felt a little tired after swimming and keeping Kaya afloat in the pool. I was doing my hair when her fingers traced my neck, sending shivers down my spine. I turned and saw Kaya sitting right behind me, feeling playful and flirting. She kept touching. Every touch was a promise, every glance a shared connection. For years, we'd been circling like two stars caught in each other's orbit, uniting on those weeks of the vacation.

Our love, affection and intimacy were fundamental to our relationship. Love served as the foundation, while my affection for Kaya served as the bond that held our relationship together and intimacy was the much-needed spark that ignited it. Every shared laugh, every accidental and intentional brush of hands and every intimate moment we shared had increased the pull between us.

She pulled me slowly, giving me time to pull away. But I didn't. Instead, I closed the gap, letting the moment out and savoring the anticipation. As our lips met, it wasn't just a joining of mouths but of souls; all her unsaid words, the pent-up feelings, were conveyed in those lingering kisses and soft bites.

All thoughts in my mind faded away as we lost ourselves in each other, our unspoken passion burning brightly within us as if nature was in tune with our emotions. She could feel the warmth of my hand against hers, my thumb gently rubbing circles. In my touch, she sensed a mixture of nervousness and genuine affection. Holding her hand felt like anchoring myself to reality, a gentle reminder that this was real, that Kaya in my bed was real. Her real self, not the Kaya she had become.

As our fingers entwined, a tender fusion of skin against skin. Her gaze caressed my face while I reveled in the warmth of her proximity, our breaths mingling in the cool midnight air. Unlike other nights, Kaya took the initiative.

She stopped, looking deep into my eyes, searching for any sign of hesitation. When I nodded, it wasn't just physical permission but a deep-seated trust that I would honor and cherish her boundaries.

As our lips met again, I couldn't help but think how much I cherished Kaya. I yearned to show her just how deeply I cared. Her skin tingled where my fingertips brushed against her, setting her nerves on fire. Her goosebumps stood visible; every kiss sent waves of warmth coursing through our veins, melting any restriction and resistance.

"Is this okay?" I whispered against her skin, my warm breath sending shivers down her spine.

She nodded, her eyes locked onto mine, conveying her desire. As our passion ignited, we surrendered to the powerful pull between us, losing ourselves in the depths of our desire. I didn't sweep Kaya off her feet or ravish her with urgency. Instead, I held her gently as if she were the most precious thing in the world.

Our hearts conveyed volumes of love as we lay intertwined in each other's arms in the quiet aftermath. No words were needed to understand the depth of our feelings.

The New Beginning and The End

As Kaya and I returned from our blissful vacation, our families gathered at my home to welcome us back. The sun had barely risen when we embarked on our journey and the early morning drive had left Kaya quite exhausted. She had slept peacefully during the journey, finding solace in dreams of our time together.

"Kaya, wake up. We've arrived home," I whispered, gently awakening her. Stepping out of the car, I began unloading our belongings from the trunk. Still drowsy, Kaya stood by my side, seeking refuge from the inevitable barrage of inquiries and well-wishes bound to come her way. She clung to my presence, perhaps unprepared to face our families' excited curiosity without me as her shield.

Before we could enter the home, my cousin intercepted us, his eyes sparkling with eagerness.

"Hey there, you two! Welcome back," he exclaimed with a knowing glint in his eye, though the full extent of his knowledge remained a well-kept secret. "Wait, you both cannot enter the home yet." He added.

As I observed, Kaya shared a warm smile with my cousin, but her expression showed a hint of shyness. Despite the impending revelations, I couldn't help but admire her graceful and poised demeanor. Her serene presence casts a calming aura, dispelling preconceived notions or expectations.

"Why? I thought you guys would be happy after seeing us after almost a month." I replied with my questions. As we approached our eagerly awaiting families, I squeezed Kaya's hand, silently reassuring her that this was the beginning of our beautiful journey together.

My cousin stood there blocking the main door and standing near him was me and Kaya, looking poised and composed. Our families quickly gathered around him, eager to begin the next chapter of our lives together. My mother came holding a pooja thali filled with colorful flowers, incense sticks and a small, glowing diya. She performed a brief but meaningful ritual with great sincerity, offering blessings for Kaya and me to have a harmonious and prosperous life together. The Aarti ceremony, typically held after a wedding, was carried out with tenderness and care. As we entered the home, I saw radiant happiness in my mother's eyes, reflecting her joy at our homecoming. I couldn't be more optimistic about our future together and am excited to start this new journey with Kaya by my side. We finally stepped across the entrance and into the warmth of our home. We settled onto the sofa in the living area, where our families encircled us, their eyes filled with curiosity and affection.

"What?" I asked, glancing at my cousins, who were wearing cunning smiles.

"You both took your sweet time." my cousin smirked, his tone filled with playful teasing. "We thought you both would return in a day or two."

I chuckled, attempting to shift the blame squarely onto Kaya's shoulders. "Well, Kaya wanted some quality alone time with me. I was ready to return the very next day."

Kaya, caught off guard and unable to respond, felt her cheeks flush with embarrassment. She attempted to hide her face behind her hands. However, the attempt was futile amidst our family's good-natured teasing.

"Enough with the teasing," my mother interjected with an affectionate scolding. "You idiots," she continued, wrapping Kaya in a loving hug before playfully slapping my shoulder.

As I shared the news of my proposal to Kaya and her wholehearted acceptance, the atmosphere in my family soared to cloud nine. Even Kaya's parents couldn't contain their tears of joy; they were genuinely thrilled for Kaya and us.

"Now that she's agreed, let's start considering the wedding date," my father suggested confidently, casting a hopeful glance at Kaya's father.

"Yes, let's do that," Kaya's father replied, his eyes glistening with happiness as he wiped away his joyful tears.

That day, we began a newfound bond between our two families. While our parents engaged in discussions, my cousins, Kaya and I retreated to my room, where we began sharing tales of our vacation and all the wonderful experiences we had gathered. Kaya, who had been somewhat reserved in front of my parents, now felt entirely at ease, trading stories and laughter with my cousins.

Although Kaya's family had plans to leave for the day, they graciously allowed her to spend more time with my family at my request. The day flashed by as Kaya and I recounted our vacation adventures and my family, in turn, entertained her with tales from my childhood and earlier years. In those moments, I could vividly picture a complete family, with Kaya becoming an integral part of the happy family.

Later that evening, following dinner, I drove Kaya back to her home. Just as she was about to step inside, I couldn't resist but express my feelings.

"I love you," I said with a soft smile. In a heartbeat, Kaya swiftly turned around, her eyes observing the surroundings, before planting a swift yet affectionate kiss on my lips. It was her delightful way of returning my heartfelt confession of love.

As I continued on my way home, excitement compelled me to dial Vijay's number and share the thrilling news with him. Vijay's heartfelt joy for us was detectable through the phone; his warm congratulations warmed my heart. After a delightful conversation, I wrapped it up by suggesting we meet at the office the following day. With that, I ended the call.

Before stepping inside my home, I paused momentarily, lighting a cigarette. Amid the tendrils of smoke, I messaged Kaya, assuring her that I had safely reached home.

In the blink of an eye, merely a month after our return from that unforgettable vacation, with the blessings of our families and the joyous cheers of our friends and relatives, Kaya and I embarked on our journey as a married couple. The wedding ceremony was a beautiful and vibrant celebration of our love, uniting us in the presence of those who held a special place in our hearts.

***

It has been five years since Kaya and I took those sacred vows, marking the beginning of our journey as a married couple and in those five years, a lot has happened.

Our world was filled with joy as we celebrated the second birthday of our beautiful daughter, Kavya. The atmosphere in our home had been electric with anticipation and excitement as we prepared for her special day. Our little princess had been dressed in a pink gown that made her look like royalty and she fluttered around the house with sparkling eyes filled with delight. Friends and family had gathered, adding to the festive ambiance with their cheerful banter and hearty laughter.

I had been grateful for my cousins' warm hospitality. They joyfully greeted guests with beaming smiles and proudly showcased our little Kavya, who had grown so much since their last visit. We had been unable to be happier to share in this delightful experience.

"Look how much she's grown!" Kaya's mother said, her eyes brimming with affection. "It's hard to believe she's already two."

"She's growing fast," Kaya's father replied, his face illuminated by paternal pride. "Watching her grow is a gift."

As the adults chatted comfortably in the cozy living room, the children were having a delightful time playing in the wide-open garden, giggling and chatting. As the moment for cake-cutting approached, Kavya had taken the spotlight, her eyes shining excitedly. Her little eyes sparkled as she saw her favorite characters on the cake. She enthusiastically sang "Happy Birthday" with all her heart, blowing out the candles. The room was filled with warmth and joyous applause, creating a truly magical atmosphere. It has been a moment to cherish and remember forever!

"It's time for presents now," Kavya declared in her childlike voice. Eagerly, she unwrapped her gifts, her gratitude expressed with a heart full of joy. Among her treasures, she had been especially thrilled with the magnificent dollhouse gifted by Kaya's father.

The celebration continued for hours. As the night drew closer, my family thanked our dear guests. The birthday celebration party had left us weary but content and it was perfect for my daughter Kavya.

It had been almost a year since I had met my former colleagues and friends from work. Payal, Vijay, Anjali and many other friends had come together to celebrate a birthday. As the evening progressed, families and close friends moved to our garden. I briefly met my friends before they left while our little one, Kavya, was busy playing with her new toys. We noticed she was getting tired, so we decided it was time for her to go to bed and get a good night's sleep.

After taking her to my room, I ensured Kavya was tucked in well for a good night's sleep. We had established a routine over the past few months; I would stay with her and tell her a couple bedtime stories before she could doze off. Kavya was a light sleeper who needed absolute silence before deep sleep. As I tried to leave the room quietly, she woke up and asked me to stay with her and continue telling her stories. She refused to sleep until I told her a few more stories.

After sharing bedtime stories with my daughter, giving her a goodnight kiss and expressing my love, I sat by her side until she drifted into dreams. Quietly closing the door, I left it slightly ajar and headed to the garden for a contemplative moment, accompanied by a cigarette. As I sat among the flowers, I sifted through pictures from that evening, capturing the undeniable resemblance between Kavya and her mother. Their shared eyes and smiles evoked a flood of memories.

Almost two blissful years had passed since Kaya and I tied the knot. The month of our wedding was a whirlwind of festivity, joy and love. Our siblings and parents radiated happiness, making the orchestrations seem like smooth sailing. The meticulous planning, from venue selection to catering, music, stage decor and lighting, was expertly handled by my cousins. Kaya and I merely had to appear when summoned for shopping.

In those days, Kaya immersed herself in wedding preparations, spending quality time with my family. Her involvement in selecting invitation cards, choosing gifts and attending to various wedding-related matters made her an integral part of my family even before the official union. Every evening, her father would pick her up from our home and on weekends, I gladly dropped her off at hers. Collaborating with my mother, Kaya transformed our bedroom into a haven filled with warmth and love.

Post-wedding, the customary honeymoon awaited us—a magical interlude inviting the newlyweds to bask in the euphoria of their union. It presented a rare opportunity to unwind, rejuvenate and deepen our connection in a serene and intimate setting, far removed from the hustle and bustle of everyday life.

When I asked Kaya where she wanted us to spend our honeymoon, her choice was unexpected but undeniably Kaya. She wished to go to her hometown, which held a special significance as her haven for her. In this place, our journey of togetherness had initially begun. Many couples explore new and distant lands during their honeymoon, eager to immerse themselves in novel cultures and experiences. However, in our case, long before our marriage, we had already ventured far and wide, discovering diverse places and embracing various cultures. What I yearned for during our honeymoon was simply Kaya's true self, Kaya, who had opened her heart to me.

A week after our wedding, we embarked on our honeymoon, heading to her hometown. The house we were going to was far from what I had previously seen. Kaya's father had lovingly renovated the house as a gift for his daughter, turning it into Kaya's cherished sanctuary. Both her father and I understood the profound significance of this house in Kaya's life. It provided her with a warmth and comfort that no other place, not even my home, could match. At one point, I suggested to Kayak that we consider moving there permanently. Yet, bearing in mind the wishes of our families and their desire to be with us, creating new joyous memories, she had gently declined that idea.

Our honeymoon week was a dreamy and romantic experience, just as it should be, brimming with love, intimacy and moments of tenderness. Upon our arrival in Kaya's hometown, we settled in and decided to take a leisurely walk around the charming town.

As evening approached, Kaya engaged in household chores and I saw the perfect opportunity to surprise her. Excitedly, I took the initiative to transform our bedroom into a space that I believed she would adore. Patiently waiting outside the bedroom, I eagerly anticipated her reaction, hoping it would be as magical as I had envisioned.

With a soft creak, the bedroom door swung open, unveiling a sight that took Kaya by surprise. The room was transformed into a romantic haven, illuminated by numerous candles' soft, flickering glow. Delicate flowers adorned the bed and their sweet scent flowed. A large mirror hung on the wall, reflecting the soft candlelight and the inviting bed.

Kaya entered the room, her eyes widening in astonishment as she took in the enchanting ambiance. She moved toward the bed, her fingers lightly tracing the rose-petal-covered sheets, which felt as soft as a cloud. Turning to me, who stood in the doorway with an eager smile, she spoke softly but with heartfelt sincerity.

"It's absolutely beautiful," she whispered, her eyes shining with appreciation. "Thank you."

I walked over to Kaya and gently took her hand in mine. "I wanted the first night of our honeymoon to be something truly special," I confessed with a warm smile. "I'm glad that you like it."

Leading her to the bed, we sat down with great care, ensuring the delicate rose petals remained undisturbed. Kaya's curious gaze wandered around the room, taking in every charming detail. The walls bore a soothing, creamy hue, while the furnishings were rich, dark wood. A generously sized window on one wall allowed the moonlight to pour in, casting a magical silver glow across the room.

On the other side of the bed, a nightstand held a softly lit lamp and a vase of freshly picked flowers, their fragrance filling the air. Kaya beamed at me, her heart full of gratitude. "It's absolutely perfect," she whispered.

Drawing closer, I tenderly kissed her. "Just like you," I murmured affectionately.

We lay together on the bed, allowing our desires to take over. The rose petals provided a delightful sensation against our skin as we snuggled closer. Kaya closed her eyes, taking a deep breath to savor the moment. Wrapped in love and happiness, she understood this was the inception of a beautiful life together. Throughout that entire week, we were in each other's company emotionally and physically.

When we eventually returned to our home in the city, our families couldn't overlook the love bites adorning our bodies. My mischievous cousin seized every chance to tease us, especially Kaya, who was already embarrassed.

***

"Son, come inside and head to bed. It's past midnight and Kavya might wake up and get upset about not finding you," my father gently urged, snapping me out of my reminiscing about Kaya and our memories.

"Please, just give me five more minutes," I requested, my voice choking with emotion.

My father nodded understandingly and exited into the house. I remained seated, reflecting on life and smoked one last cigarette before calling it a night. After extinguishing the cigarette, I went inside, showered and settled into bed. The stress of the past two years had left me battling insomnia and I lay there with my eyes closed, craving for the comfort of sleep to wash over me.

"Daddy, where is Mama?" Kavya's innocent voice pierced the stillness of the night as she woke up, her curiosity piqued about Kaya's whereabouts. "You said she'd come for my birthday."

Kavya had seen Kaya in the photo only. She never received her mother's love; no matter how much we showered her with love, we were not Kaya, a mother she longed for.

I hugged her gently, whispering, "She'll be here soon," not having the heart to reveal that Kaya was no longer with us. None of us in the family dared to explain the concept of death to her or what it meant for her. Kavya's innocent questions and yearning for her mother's warmth were heart-wrenching.

Sometimes, she would ask, "You have your mother and you live with her, but I don't." I usually found myself at a loss for words to answer her innocent questions. As I tried to soothe her back to sleep, I found myself drifting into memories of Kaya, unable to escape the pain in my heart. I remembered the day I heard the news of us being pregnant with Kavya like it was just yesterday.

***

I was in an important meeting during a busy evening in the office, but my mind couldn't focus. I kept looking at my phone, expecting a call from my family. Both Kaya and my mother were at the hospital. Once the meeting ended, I immediately dialed Kaya's number, but they were still waiting at the hospital.

"Why do you keep calling me?" Kaya asked with frustration, "I told you our appointment isn't until six o'clock."

"Please, just call me as soon as you speak to the doctor and find out anything," I replied, eager to get updates as soon as possible.

Kaya and I were ready and excited to start a family, but somehow, we were not able to conceive and get pregnant. As months passed, our fear and frustration grew; it was overwhelming, especially for Kaya. We had tried the conventional methods to maximize our chances; we tried having frequent intercourse during her fertile window, tracking her temperature every morning and using technology like predictor kits and ovulation tracker apps, but nothing helped.

A year passed and still, we couldn't get pregnant. Deep down, we suspected the reason but decided it was time to seek medical help rather than guessing. Kaya's episodes had added to her struggles to become a mother, but we were determined to find a solution. Kaya was desperate to attain motherhood and we did everything we could. When Kaya missed her period, it gave us hope; my mother had accompanied Kaya to her doctor's appointment, where we hoped to get answers and a path forward. It was a beacon of hope for us.

After about an hour, my phone rang and Kaya called. She and my mother were returning home from the doctor's appointment.

"The tests are positive," Kaya said, her voice filled with tears of joy and relief. "We're going to have a baby."

Hearing those words was like a dream come true for me. "Thank you, Kaya!" I shouted, not caring that I was in the office. I was over the moon. "I love you!"

The news of our upcoming parenthood was the perfect reward for all our efforts and struggles. My colleagues joined the celebration, congratulating me as I left work early that day.

Those nine months were the most important months of our life. No matter how much we tried, Kaya's past wouldn't go away; she continued to have episodes where she would have nightmares. They were getting worse; some days, she was just getting nightmares reliving her painful past and some days, she would cry remembering her younger sister.

We needed a solution and fast. After careful discussion and consideration, I suggested to everyone that until the delivery, Kaya should stay at her hometown home. It was the only place where she could feel comfortable and safe. The families agreed with my suggestions and Kaya and I stayed at her hometown house. Our mothers would take turns visiting us in the hometown, ensuring Kaya wasn't unattended for a single day or night.

As months passed, the pregnancy and her stress were taking a toll on her health, but thanks to the care provided by the families and the warmth of her hometown home, we could go through the last four months of pregnancy without any major complications. During the doctor's visit, we learned that the baby was safe and healthy and it was almost time for us to hold the baby we all had been nurturing for months. Everyone in the family was very happy with the news and anticipation of the baby. Few longed for a baby girl and others wanted a baby boy. After hearing the news from the doctor that everything was normal and the baby had grown well in her care, Kaya was happiest.

After a week, Kaya started feeling labor pain and we got her admitted to the hospital. Those two days, both families were eagerly waiting for the news. Kaya was feeling anxious as her water had broken and the doctor had asked her to wait patiently; we were expecting the arrival of a baby anytime soon. Kaya was taken into the labor room and we learned that looking at Kaya's health condition, it would be best to go for a C-section. I signed the consent form, giving the hospital and doctor permission to perform the procedure.

The anxiety was eating me up and it was hard for me to control my nerves; I stepped outside the office and smoked. The same evening, our daughter Kavya was born. The birth of our daughter would change everything for us, especially for Kaya; that is what I had thought, but my dream of making new memories with Kaya and our daughter was short-lived.

A week after we became parents, Kaya's situation started worsening; the episodes were more frequent and more painful than ever. The medication wasn't working at all and every attempt I made to make her feel safe and happy wasn't helping. Kaya started isolating herself from others and our newborn daughter.

Some nights, Kaya would wake up in the middle of the night and stay awake crying, consumed by the fear of having painful nightmares. Others, she would sleep like a completely normal mother caring for her newborn. Our families were getting worried about her and our daughter. The cycle continued for several months and it was becoming difficult for Kaya to cope with it.

One night, when I was sitting in our bedroom looking at Kavya sleeping, Kaya came and sat before me. She sat there without saying anything and kept looking at something in the distance.

"What are you thinking about?" I asked her while holding her hand.

"Do you remember our first vacation?" She asked while smiling.

"Of course, I do. How can I forget that?" I replied to her with a smile. "Why are you asking me about our vacation suddenly? I was curious to know the reason behind that question

"Do you also remember the promises you made?" She added.

"We made many promises on that vacation, Kaya. Which one are you talking about." I replied to her. The gentle smile I had vanished; I had made many promises to Kaya, some I was ready to keep and some I wasn't.

"The promise where you would never ask me any question when I asked to live at my hometown home alone." She replied with tears in her eyes.

I remembered the entire discussion around that promise with every word like it had happened just yesterday. I couldn't forget that discussion and the promise I made. "No, I can't leave you alone," I replied with a heavy heart. "Not in your current condition."

The abrupt end of my dream, with the haunting image of Kaya leaving me, jolted me awake. I hurried to the garden, tears streaming down my face. The pain of Kaya's loss overwhelmed me.

In the aftermath of Kaya's death, I descended into a profound despair, losing all hope and succumbing to a numbing slumber. My family shouldered the responsibility of caring for our daughter as I grappled with grief. Unable to contain my emotions around them, I opted for isolation, embarking on a journey to Kaya's hometown, the place where she drew her last breath.

Within the walls of her family home, I sensed Kaya's lingering presence, as if she played a perpetual game of hide and seek. However, I understood that her spirit eluded my human eyes. The burden of guilt weighed heavily on me, knowing that Kaya's demise in that house was, in part, due to my decision to let her live there alone when she needed me the most. I should have stayed by her side, attuned to the struggles within her mind.

Grief became an oppressive shroud, enveloping my heart and soul. Its weight made every breath a struggle, every thought a challenge. I carried it with me everywhere, a relentless reminder of the love I had lost. Regrets echoed in my mind – not staying with Kaya, not preventing her departure, not expressing my love more profoundly. I had assumed time was abundant, but a single day shattered that illusion. Now, I grapple with the irreparable guilt of knowing I could have saved her, but she is gone, irrevocably.

Nearly a year immersed in mourning Kaya's death led me back to our daughter, Kavya. It marked both a new beginning and an ending. A fresh start for Kavya and me to forge a life together, creating joyful memories, while simultaneously concluding my mourning for Kaya. The memory of her will never fade and forgiving myself might prove elusive, but I had to keep living. For our daughter, Kavya and the dreams Kaya left unfulfilled, I vowed to carry on and shape a future filled with happiness.

The Letter

As I write this, I struggle to encapsulate a lifetime of emotions into mere words. This letter is the hardest I've ever had to write, not because I lack the words, but because I have so much to say and apologize for and so little time left.

Do you remember those lazy afternoons when time seemed to stand still just for us? We laughed so much that our sounds resonated through the walls while our shared dreams painted pictures in the air. Those moments were my haven, my sanctuary. Being with you made me incredibly happy, to the point where I was often breathless. Your love shone like a beacon that cut through the darkness of my toughest nights, bringing a warmth and light I can't put into words. Our love story was filled with beauty and passion despite its challenges. Each day spent with you was a precious chapter in the story of my life that I will always cherish. These memories, our shared laughter and the love surrounding us are the treasures I hold closest to my heart.

When I reflect on the days spent in my hometown after becoming a mother, those memories are tinted with a bittersweet hue. Motherhood was a dream I had always cherished, yet the reality was far more challenging than I ever anticipated. The joys were unparalleled, but so were the trials. I was navigating a maze of new emotions, responsibilities and the rekindling of old pains I thought I had long buried.

You see, my past, filled with its share of pain and suffering, never really left me. It lingered like a shadow, shaping my thoughts and actions in ways I didn't fully understand. And in the midst of it all, I realize now I failed to see the impact it was having on you and our newborn daughter. For that, I am deeply sorry.

I've always believed in facing life's challenges head-on, but in doing so, I inadvertently built walls around myself. Walls that not only protected me but also isolated me from the ones I loved the most – you and our daughter. In my effort to be strong, to not burden you with my past and my pain, I ended up instilling pain in you instead. I see that now and it breaks my heart.

There were days when the weight of my memories and the effort of putting up a brave front for the world left me exhausted. I wanted to share my burden with you, but I didn't know how. I was afraid that showing my vulnerabilities would somehow diminish the strength you saw in me. That fear kept me silent and in that silence, I realized I had drifted further away from you.

But please know this - every decision I made, flawed as some may have been, stemmed from a place of love. Love for you, love for our daughter. My heart swelled with joy every time I saw her smile, every time I held her in my arms. She was and always will be, a part of me. And you, you were my anchor, my constant in a life that saw too many changes too soon.

I am sorry for the pain I caused and the times I let my suffering cloud our happiness. As I face these final moments, I only hope you find it in your heart to forgive me. I leave this world full of love for you and our daughter and a soul filled with regret for not being the wife and mother you deserved.

There is one final request I must entrust to you. Our daughter, the light of our lives, must never bear the weight of my past. Please, I implore you to let her remain unaware of the darkness and pain that once clouded my life. She deserves to grow in the warmth of love, untainted by the shadows over me. Promise me that you will fill her days with joy, laughter and stories of love, not of the struggles I endured. I want her to know of the strength and happiness we found together, not the sorrow that preceded it. As for my part, I will watch over both of you wherever I may be, showering her with all my love. Let my legacy in her life be one of unending love and care – a love that encompasses both of us. She is our precious daughter, a testament to our love and she should only ever know the brightness of life, not the storms I weathered.

Take care of our little girl. Tell her about me, us and the love that brought her into this world. And most importantly, live a life full of the joy and happiness I couldn't give you. You both deserve that and so much more.

Love you.

Kaya